M000074538

Sara Gallardo

January

Translated from the Spanish by
Frances Riddle and Maureen Shaughnessy

archipelago books

Library of Congress Cataloging-in-Publication Data available upon request.
ISBN: 9781953861641

Archipelago Books
232 3rd Street #A111
Brooklyn, NY 11215
www.archipelagobooks.org

Distributed by Penguin Random House
www.penguinrandomhouse.com

Cover art: Max Kahn
Book design: Zoe Guttenplan

This work is made possible by the New York State Council on the Arts with the support of
the Office of the Governor and the New York State Legislature. Funding for the publication
of this book was provided by a grant from the Carl Lesnor Family Foundation.

This publication was made possible with support from Lannan Foundation,
the Jan Michalski Foundation, the National Endowment for the Arts,
Programa SUR, and the New York City Department of Cultural Affairs.

PRINTED IN THE UNITED STATES

January

For Luis Pico Estrada

1

They talk about the harvest but they don't know that by then there'll be no turning back, Nefer thinks. Everyone here and everywhere else will know by then, and they won't be able to stop talking about it. Her eyes cloud with worry; she slowly lowers her head and herds a small flock of crumbs across the worn oilcloth. Her father mentions the harvest and then reaches for the tea towel used to wipe all the hands and mouths around the table. Her mother stands to pass it to him, stepping on the dog, which yelps and takes refuge under the bench. As she walks, her shadow moves across those of the people seated around the table, held fixed on the walls by the light of a lantern. The day will come when my belly starts to show,

Nefer thinks. The insects buzz, flutter, and fall as they hit the lantern. They climb back up the lantern's tin skirt, singe their wings and fall back down again. No one pays any attention to her, still and silent in the corner, as they lean over their plates eating and listening to the occasional exchange between Don Pedro and the Turk, who slurps a spoonful of soup, still out of breath after unhitching his horses from the cart.

"Holsteins," the Turk says. "About a hundred head . . . Good-looking cows."

"Where did you say you passed them, Nemi?" Doña María asks.

"Near the crossing. On their way to the market, I reckon . . ."

"That's right, the market's tomorrow . . . But whose could they be? . . . You don't know, do you, Juan? Who was planning to sell cattle tomorrow?"

Juan yawns, not hearing her as he stares into the lantern with bleary eyes.

"Juan!"

"Yes, ma'am!" Juan is new to his job on the ranch and doesn't want to look dumb.

"I was asking you who might be sending cattle to the market, the Turk saw some Holsteins . . ."

Nefer measures the distance between her body and the table, thinking how before long she won't be able to slip past and sit at the end of the bench. But by then I won't be coming to meals. By then I might be dead. And she pictures herself surrounded by flowers and sad faces, and Negro leaning in the doorway with a serious expression, finally laying his eyes on her. But even then he'll probably be looking at Alcira, she thinks, discouraged, and her desire to die fades as she watches her sister pensively scratch her arm while she waits for the Turk to finish eating so she can clear his plate.

Shadows dance along the rough wall and merge with the darkness of the roof where the thatch stretches like a taut braid. Alcira turns on the radio and tunes from station to station until stopping on a comedy show with a voice screeching in a fake Italian accent.

Don Pedro resumes his conversation with the Turk, the radio like a waterfall drowning out their voices.

"So, it was expensive, huh?"

"Sure was, but like I said, if we get a good harvest it'll be cheaper in the end . . ."

The harvest, impossible for it to come without everyone knowing. A howl rises in her throat but stops at her teeth, sliding back down to where it came from. She longs for a moment of fresh air, to get out of this kitchen where the heat from the lantern laps at their faces and the air vibrates with the hum of the radio and Doña María laughs with Alcira at the actors' jokes.

But to leave she would first have to ask everyone else on the bench to stand, and also explain why she wants to go outside. No, better not to call attention to herself; maybe a sip of wine will make her feel better. She reaches for the bottle that Don Pedro has just set down, brings it to her lips and closes her eyes as she drinks. Then she pushes open the little window beside her and a waft of fresh air hits her face. She leans out to look for the lights of Santa Rosa Ranch in the distance, but all she can see is the foliage of a nearby tree.

If only Negro knew that it's his, that it's his, then maybe he'd notice me, maybe he'd love me and marry me. Maybe the three of us could all ride off in a buggy to live the rest of our lives on another ranch, far away from here.

But it's not his . . . Yes, yes it is, it's his . . . No, it's not . . . But it *is* Negro's fault, it's definitely his fault. What's a young woman to do? All alone in the country, a countryside so vast and green, nothing but horizon, with trains going off to cities and coming back from who knows where. What can she do?

It's a different story for rich girls. She thinks of Luisa, who at this time of night must be sitting at the dining table in the estancia. Nefer's mother once said, "Those girls are all the same, they can roll in the hay with whoever they like and no one will find out. They have their ways." Is that true? But dear God, what about me? What have I done? Nothing, it was nothing, she hardly even remembers it, it didn't matter, it was like a dream, and now, seated among all these carefree people living their lives, she feels only worry and fear.

Because there's no going back, time keeps passing and everything grows, and after growth comes death. But you can never go backwards.

And Negro, when he finds out, when Edilia hears about it – that sharp tongue of hers, that laugh of hers – Negro might smile, might even make a joke . . . No, oh no, and it's all *his* fault, it's Negro's fault, because she doesn't even know how it happened, but it's all Negro's fault.

She thinks about how she might have never even met him, and then it's as if she's been transported back to the day she first saw him. She feels the lightness in the air again, the fresh breeze. The entire family had gone to the rodeo because it had been a while since the prizes were so big. Her cousin, a pale, skinny, bowlegged fellow, had a good shot at winning. Nefer remembers squinting to see him mount his horse, then his body swaying in the saddle, one arm held up timidly in the air, too scared to crack the whip.

From behind her someone had said: "He's gonna make off with quite a prize if he keeps whipping that horse so hard . . ."

The joke was met with several laughs. Nefer, humiliated for her cousin's sake, turned her head in contempt to confront the wise-cracker, but when she saw him, with one leg crossed casually over the saddlebow, a cigarette in his mouth, she looked down. That was the first time she'd ever laid eyes on Negro Ramos, but his fame as a horseman preceded him.

"Nefer! Someone's talking to you! You'd think she's dim! Are you falling asleep?"

She looks up to see the Turk, Nemi Bleis, his bushy mustache leaning toward her. And she stares at the web of veins crisscrossing his nose to avoid thinking about how long he might have been speaking to her before she noticed.

"What were you saying?" she asks.

"About that fabric I sold you the last time I came through, for your sister's wedding; the floral print, remember? How'd it turn out?"

"Yes, of course. It turned out real nice, thank you."

Real nice indeed, Porota's wedding, where all her troubles began. How could she forget the party? That house, the hot day, the fire pits between the barn and the corral, how Negro had shown up on the sorrel horse he was breaking in. She'd been looking forward to Porota's wedding because of him, she'd sewn that new dress for him, and even before, when the Turk came through with his wares, she'd chosen that floral fabric because she thought Negro would like it.

Mending sweaty bombachas ripped from so much rubbing in the stirrups is a chore; darning shirts is dull, but a dress — a dress you've made a pattern for and tried on a thousand times, unstitched and reworked until its final form takes shape in your hands – a dress is something else.

She remembers how carefully she'd pressed the dress, filling the iron with hot coals and then taking it out to the yard for the breeze to revive it.

If the patrones of El Retiro Ranch hadn't called a priest to come out and give a special Mass for some saint, the bride and groom would've had to get married in town. They would've gone by bus, on a Wednesday, all solemn, carrying Porota's dress on a hanger. But since the priest was coming they could get married in the chapel across from the general store, and the reception could be held at the house.

While Nefer stayed home to iron her dress, Porota and Alcira had gone into town to perm their hair and they came back looking like little lambs. She remembers it well; she'd pressed that dress so carefully. Thinking about it now makes her want to cry.

All day she'd waited, until suddenly, flanked by two or three other riders, she saw him appear with a big silver knife across his waist. The trotting of his horse jingled the coins on his shiny belt and Nefer, ah, there was Nefer, serving mate for the guests alongside her sister. She didn't look; she turned her back and scalded her hand with the water she was pouring, but she listened – for a while she was nothing more than a pair of ears — as he dismounted, tied up his horse, and joked with his friends; she heard his footsteps cross the yard before he came in to greet everyone in the kitchen. When it was her turn she answered quickly: goodandyou, and then offered him the mate, lowering her gaze.

Lunch came, serving the guests, coming and going, the heat, the coals throbbing in the dirt next to the spits dripping fat, the men bending over to slowly carve the meat. There had been wine and empanadas — rolling out dough for hours the night before with her mother and cousins. The sun beat down on the dirt yard, everyone's faces were red in the shade of the hackberry trees, then Jacinto started to play the accordion and lively music filled the morning air. But she, Nefer, with the plate of empanadas or the tray of meat, Nefer, with the wine or splitting the hardtack, had eyes in the back of her head, up and down her arms, her neck, all over her body. Without looking at him directly, she could see Negro the whole time. She watched him huddled among some friends, eating meat with his big knife, one bite and then another, nimbly and leisurely smiling and talking.

The whole day went on like that, with Negro at the center of it all. But right beside Negro was Delia.

If only Nefer's nails had not been worn down to the nubs from so much work; if she had not been the sister of the bride; if instead she had been someone else, she would have ripped Delia's face to shreds, silencing that squawking laugh of hers! She would have ground her hateful body into the dirt, tied her hair to the tail of a colt, strung her up naked by her feet over the fire. And once Delia was charred and destroyed, Nefer would have fed her ashes to the caracaras, to the dogs, to the possums, to the foxes. Ah, Delia, a shop owner's daughter, at ease, pampered.

Like a pale scar that suddenly burns red with exertion, her grand-mother's blood flared up in her veins. Nefer had barely known the woman and yet she lived on inside her. The grandmother who wandered the Carhué lagoons and the sandy fields of the Indian encampments to the west; the dark-skinned grandmother who died at the age of one hundred without a hint of gray, a terrifying wisdom in her words. Mamá never spoke of the woman because her own bloodline had come from Italy on both sides. Papá felt no need to mention his mother, nor did her granddaughters.

What is a day? What is the world when everything inside you shudders? The sky darkens, houses swell, merge, topple, voices rise in unison to become a single sound. Enough! Who is that shouting? Her soul is black, a soul like the fields in a storm, without a single ray of light, silent as a corpse in the ground.

Nefer passes around the mate. There's dancing in the barn and she takes turns with several fellows under the bright light of the lanterns. Then she runs, flees. Nicolás, who works on the railroad – an enormous man – stands in her path and says, "Nefer."

She stops.

"What do you have there? mate?"

Nefer looks at him but she doesn't see his face, she doesn't see his mustache, all she sees is Delia and Negro, dancing and laughing. She says yes. She could've just as easily said no. The man says:

"Can I have some? I'm thirsty."

"It's all out. I have to change it."

Tears run down her cheeks, but she doesn't know it. The man reeks of wine, she'd seen him laughing and talking all afternoon.

He takes her by the arm, past the tree line, and the brambles stick into her back. The man has a mustache, he smells of wine, it's hot, the branches of the trees are a world unto themselves. Negro is with Delia, the man is sweaty, it's hot, I'm suffocating. Oh Negro, Negro, what have you done to me? Look at my dress, it was supposed to be for you. I've been waiting months for this day to finally talk to you . . .

Bottles clink as Don Pedro pushes the table back so the Turk can stand up. Dinner is over and Juan gets up murmuring "thanks for the meal" as he picks his teeth with the point of his knife. Nefer waits for the bench to empty before she slides out; her mother pours boiling water into a tub full of soapy plates and knives and forks that Alcira then dries and puts away. Nefer wipes the table with a rag in slow circles, herding crumbs to the edge, letting them fall to the ground for the dogs and chickens to fight over.

"Let's find something else on the radio," her mother says, because the comedy program has given way to some dramatic music followed by a soap opera heavy with sighs.

"Wait," says Alcira. "Leave it here. It's Claudia Reyes."

Nefer moves away from the radio and turns back to her rag, but she quickly drops it and rushes out into the night where she grabs hold of a tree and vomits. A jolt of pain contorts her; her eyes cloud, her throat burns, anguish throbs in her ears. Far away, a train glides endlessly over the shadowy plains.

Dying, she thinks, would be better. She sighs, her desperation merging with the whispering of the trees. She watches as Nemi Bleis carries his bedding into the room where Juan is undressing by candlelight, and Don Pedro disappears around the side of the house for one last check before turning in. The light thrown onto the yard by the open kitchen door is suddenly blocked by a thick shadow.

"Nefer!" Doña María shouts. "Nefer!"

"Coming!"

Before going inside she turns her head and looks over the horizon toward the unwavering light of Santa Rosa, where Negro must be finishing his dinner. Farther west, the stands of trees rise up protectively around the little homesteads, which one by one turn out their lights and dissolve into the plains.

2

She'd rather stand outside in the soft morning light, waiting for the patrona to appear with her endless clattering of words, not inside the kitchen where all those people will offer her things and make her sit.

She thinks that today this thing filling her up inside, choking her, might turn against her, pound at the walls, so she prefers to wait outside leaning against a tree. There she stands in the dirt that stretches monotonously beneath her feet out to the horizon, and she lets her eyes rest on every hair, every swirl in the fur of the dog she is petting.

No further. Not into the garden and its flowers, not over the fields or past the windows of the house to see if anyone is looking: nothing beyond this immediate moment.

The cook comes out:

"Hey!" she shouts, "the patrona says for you to come in, to wait for her inside!"

"No thank you," Nefer answers quietly, "I'm fine here, I'm . . ."

"Come on, I'll give you some bread and butter. What're you doing out there with that dog? Don't be stubborn, child."

She abandons the dog and approaches, the stick she's been using as a riding crop tucked under her arm.

"What's that? Leave it outside, I don't need any junk in here."

She drops the stick and goes in. She knows the smell of that kitchen, with the maid darning socks beside the window, the butler polishing silverware like a pale impassive post, the cook with a checkered apron stretched over her fat belly.

"Good morning," she murmurs.

"Morning."

"Sit down, child."

She's an outsider in this big red kitchen where she has been summoned by her godmother, Doña Mercedes. What for? She no longer cares about anything besides this thing that consumes her days and nights, growing inside her like a dark mushroom, and she wonders if it shows in her eyes as they remain fixed on her worn-out espadrilles, two little gray boats on the tile floor, or in her hands crossed in her lap, or in her hair burned by the perm.

"Are you Alcira, Porota, or the other one?" the maid asks.

"I'm Nefer."

"You're looking pale, you know. And skinny . . . You could learn a thing or two from your sister."

Nefer smiles weakly – a sad, faint smile – and looks down at her leathery hands, clasped tightly as if consoling one another.

"Which of the patronas called for you?"

"Doña Mercedes, she told me to come by today."

"Oh, because the older one's sick. Here, eat this, let's see if we can get a little color into those cheeks of yours."

"Thanks."

The door opens and Luisa walks in with a handkerchief tied around her neck and a book in her hand. "Morning," she says. "How are you, Nefer?"

"Goodandyou, Luisa."

"Good morning, Miss Luisa," the butler says didactically.

She sits down at the table and crosses her legs. She's wearing pants that – as Nefer's father says – make her look like a lapwing.

"How is everyone on the homestead?" she asks.

"They're fine, thanks. They send their greetings."

"Thank you. Is your father working on my new whip?"

"No – I don't know."

"I'll take that as a no. I'll have to go by and remind him."

"Of course, you're always welcome," Nefer smiles.

"Excuse me, do you have the time?" Luisa asks.

"It's ten o'clock, miss."

"Oh, good. I still have some time. See you later," and she leaves.

Nefer smiles again. She often sees Luisa gallop past the outpost surrounded by a pack of dogs.

She eats slowly and the taste of the butter gives her a ray of hope.

"Oh, child, you could wash your hands before you eat," says the maid. "Look how filthy." And Nefer notices her five black fingernails framing the crust of bread.

Doña Mercedes's voice precedes her and Nefer rushes to swallow. When the door opens she clumsily sets the bread on the oilcloth and stands up. Doña Mercedes walks in like a globe with two pink parentheses as arms.

"How are you, my child?" she says. "Go on, eat up. Your family's doing well? You had a birthday recently, didn't you? How old are you now?"

"I turned sixteen, ma'am."

"Sixteen, that's right. Alcira's eighteen, correct? And Porota? How is she? Is she in the family way yet?"

"I don't know, ma'am."

The lady has been in the garden and her shoes are caked in mud. A pure sort of mud, Nefer thinks, somehow strangely clean.

"Three months since she got married, there should be news soon, don't you think?" The lady laughs and places a hand bearing two rings against her large bosom.

"Well . . ." says the cook, "you have to be careful, the cost of living . . ." with a peal of laughter that sounds like ten pots clanging to the floor. The butler stands up haughtily and leaves the room; the lady mocks him with a wink and continues her chatter: "Everyone's doing well, then? So, I got you this little gift for your birthday. I am your godmother after all."

"Thank you, ma'am," Nefer murmurs, not daring to look at the soft parcel in her hands. "You shouldn't have gone to the trouble."

"It's no trouble, it's my pleasure. The mission starts tomorrow. Have you heard?" Nefer's heart feels heavy. "Your mother knows already. I went by – oh, of course, you were there. Everyone will attend, I imagine. Well, you already know. Do you have to start work early? You do the milking, right?"

"Yes, ma'am."

"Well then, you can have something to drink for breakfast before communion. To *drink*, you hear me? No hardtack; something hot – café con leche or mate so you don't feel weak. Your mother and I have already talked about it. I don't know which priest will be coming but

◦ 19 ◦

I'm sure he'll be good, they always are. You've had your first communion, right? Yes, I remember now. Well, let's all behave like good
Christians, hmm? It's only once a year we have the good fortune of
hosting Our Lord right here, after all."

Nefer feels like the room is spinning as she grips the rustling
package in her hands. The rules of etiquette instilled by her mother
forbid her from opening it. One must show gratitude for a gift regard-
less of what it is. But Doña Mercedes wants to see her reaction. The
patrona takes the package, unties it on the table, and unfurls a red
knit sweater with glass buttons.

"What do you think? Do you like it?"

Nefer thinks it's sublime but knows not to show it.

"Yes, ma'am, thank you." She'll wear it tomorrow, she thinks, so
Negro can see it . . . But then the shadow looms, the black mushroom
swells inside her, rising to her throat, as she watches the lady measure
the sleeve against her arm.

"Now won't you look lovely," the cook says as Doña Mercedes
rewraps the package and Nefer stands blankly with her arms hanging
at her sides, hardly noticing.

She leaves, slowly picking her way through the thistles. Her eyes linger on the dusty, brushlike horse's mane. She looks at its impassive,

docile ears, then back down to its withers, where a rough tuft of hair hangs over his neck.

Before, when she was happy – she now knows that she had been happy before – her eyes would wander far away, from the tree line to the wind pump to a herd of horses in the distance, a buggy on the road. Not anymore, now her eyes are as heavy as her soul, and if asked what she can see she would say only my hand, the reins, a fork, a plate, and nothing beyond that. But in truth she doesn't even see those things. She sees nothing at all.

She carries the package in front of her on the sheepskin where it crinkles with every step the horse takes. She passes countless hoof prints on the road that the wind erases like a huge hand wiping them away. The ears of the dapple-gray horse twitch at the sound of an automobile that kicks up a trail of dust as an arm waves out the window. Luisa, Nefer thinks, on her way to buy cigarettes . . . and she watches as her horse's hooves speed up in agitation along the road.

She dismounts when she reaches the gate: held shut by a rough branch that has been rubbed smooth by wire. She pulls it open and sidesteps the mud churned up in the night by the cows from the milking yard. In the yellow-green field the lapwings shriek and flutter and the pond gleams in the sun, prickly with reeds.

Nefer hops back onto the horse. Then she remembers an idea she had the night before and digs in her heels. Maybe if I gallop hard. The trees loom at the end of the trail and to avoid them she turns into the field of thistles. She gallops among the sleeping cows, her legs scratched up by the thistles, dodging anthills, terrifying the partridges who rise up with whispering wings and shriek in fright. The horse is lazy, but she urges him on with her heels, gripping the package in one hand and commanding the reins with the other. The horse picks up into a gallop as they splash through the shallow pond, water glistening on her legs and face and coating the horse's mane with droplets. The twigs of duraznillos break with a snapping sound and the reeds sway their heads as she passes. Her galloping muddles the water and then the horse's hooves clomp against dry land when she emerges on the other side.

Nefer turns toward the homestead and her teeth flash into a smile: she's forgotten why she'd been galloping and she laughs, out of breath, "You're getting fat, you old horse. Are you worn out?" The lapwings trace circles in the air and shriek all around her.

Nemi's wagon is near the barn, packed and ready to leave like a little red and blue house on wheels. The Turk is putting away a suitcase, and through the open door Nefer sees the shelves inside the wagon lined with boxes and folded clothes.

"You're leaving, sir...?"

"Yes. Too bad you're just getting here now. Your sister had a look, lots of pretty things. You don't need anything? I have some combs that won't ruin your hair, fine things."

"No thanks, I don't need anything right now. Did she buy anything?"

"Some thread, real nice, white thread ..."

The Turk closes the door, turns the key in the lock, spits, and grinds the spit into the dust with his espadrille. Nefer remembers the time he told them stories of his homeland, how a saint performed the miracle of filling his own tomb with blood. "You call us Turks but the Turks are our worst enemies," he'd said. "My entire family had their throats slit by Turks. How about that?"

He's rich, according to Doña María, he has a shop in the city and spends the year traveling the countryside with his merchandise. He carries a revolver with him in the wagon and at the end of his journey he returns home with several thousand pesos.

Watching him pack up, Nefer feels a kind of tenderness for the man.

"And where are you headed now, Bleis?" she asks.

"I'm going to see if I can keep going a little longer. It's gotten late, already. One of the horses," he pats it, "ran off to the big field and it took a long time to find him. Who knows what he was after ..."

Nefer dismounts and pulls off the sheepskin. Juan walks up.

"Don't let him loose, Nefer, I need him . . ."

"What's that package?" Alcira shouts from an assembly of hens. "Did they give you something?"

Nefer unwraps the sweater, creased with newness.

"Hmmm," Doña María murmurs, "nice . . . Must have cost her a pretty penny, don't you think?"

"Who knows . . ." Alcira says. "What do they care about a few extra pesos? I like the color. But I wonder, why would she say red looks good on me and then turn around and give you something red?"

"Well . . . she's my godmother."

"Uh-huh," says her mother, wiping her hands on her apron. "Tell me something . . . was that you who threw up last night?"

"Who? Me? . . . Why would I throw up?"

"Because one of the whips got left out and it was soiled this morning. . ."

"And why blame it on me? . . . It could've been a dog, couldn't it? Or anyone else . . ."

"I don't know, it's just you've been acting strange. I don't know what bug bit you . . . But I need you to go out and buy some meat now, we don't have anything for lunch . . ."

Something lights up inside Nefer, maybe Negro is still lingering at the store, killing time. Maybe she'll run into him . . . Afraid of the answer, she asks: "Wasn't Juan just going out?"

"No, Juan has to stay here and fix the table leg . . . What're you doing?" she asks as Juan rides up on the dapple horse. "Where do you think you're off to? . . . Weren't you going to fix the table?"

"Sorry, ma'am? Didn't you say you needed some meat . . . ?"

"Well, yes, but Nefer can go. What am I supposed to do with a broken table leg?"

"All right, ma'am whatever you say. As you like." He silently dismounts, handing the reins and riding crop to Nefer.

"Hold on a minute, Juan, I'll be right back."

Nefer goes inside to look at herself in the mirror. She pulls her comb out of a dried cow's tail on the wall and passes it through the un-permed part of her hair; she looks at herself for another moment, skeptical, and then goes into the kitchen and comes back out with a bag tucked under one arm.

"Ready . . ." she takes the reins and crop from Juan's hand and jumps on the horse.

"One more thing, Nefer," he says, "a pack of Particulares if you don't mind, unfiltered." He takes out the money, counts it, and hands it to her. "Thanks."

Nefer knows that Juan's hopes of getting to chat for a while at the store have sadly faded.

"Bye," she says, kicks the horse, urging him into a gallop, and leaves.

The plains are a calm green sea under the sun and the trees beyond stretch up like a fleet of ships. Town is a dark spot at the end of the road, consisting of two shops and a few houses that have sprung up around the station. Nefer sees several dairy carts departing like toy boats with their owners at the masts. She recognizes them by the direction they take and by the horses, and she recalculates her chance of seeing Negro. Slim, because generally it's his brother who brings the milk to town, and because it's already late. If only they took the milk straight to the factory instead of the train, she'd have a better chance.

The ditches alongside the road are full of water from the recent rains and a small herd of horses graze, stepping in and out of the trenches. The animals, skinny and neglected, belong to three Basque brothers who live on a small plot of land. To save on hay, they let the horses roam free. Nefer feels sorry for the family, despite the fact that her mother can't stop criticizing them. Not long ago a neighbor poisoned one of their dogs and they took revenge by castrating all of his dogs.

Crazy Basques, she thinks. What's wrong with them? She pulls a little clump of wool from the shearling, puts it in her mouth and chews. It's a habit her father has tried to break her of but she does it when he can't see; it's not often they're on horseback together. It was ten years ago now that Don Pedro had the riding accident that sent him to the hospital and since then, by unspoken right, he stopped working. "Don Pedro's never been the same," people say, and it lends an aura of prestige to his thin dark figure drinking mate in the kitchen. Some days he saddles up the horse and rides to the general store, where he drinks and chats politely, but he normally stays out on the homestead, preparing strips of rawhide and braiding leather with his hands that resemble gnarled roots. He's often called on to diagnose and cure ailing horses as well.

Nefer admires her father and fears her mother, whose body is three times the size of Don Pedro's. Alcira is going to turn out like their mother, she thinks, and the thought cheers her up.

Several caracaras pick silently at a carcass sticking out of the water in the ditch. Poor creature. She tries to imagine the sensation of falling exhausted beside the road, with no strength left to react to the cowhands' shouts and whips, eyes closing to die as the mooing of the herd and the whistles fade away, left alone in the night with the crickets, the lightning bugs, and the barking of faraway dogs.

Poor creature, she thinks again as she reaches town on the dusty road and some puppies run out of the first house to yip at her. The horse turns automatically toward the general store, with Luisa's car parked out front, but Nefer urges him on to the butcher shop, a tin house across from the station. She dismounts hoping there won't be too many people. She noticed that Negro's cart was not parked outside the general store when she passed.

Another day lived for nothing, she thinks as she pushes open the screen door to the butcher's. When she enters, a few other customers waiting in uncomfortable silence return her gaze.

"G'morning . . ." she says with half a voice.

". . . G'morning . . ."

"Mornin'. . ."

She always has the same suffocating feeling in this little shop, with its sickly-sweet air, slabs of meat hanging from the ceiling, and the greasy counter. The daylight that filters in through the screened windows seems unreal and she can't tell whether the flies are crawling inside or out. A tall, silent Basque man watches the butcher prepare his order and a whiskered old man waits with a cigarette hanging from his lips and his beret pulled down to his eyes. A girl stands beside Nefer, staring at the floor; they were classmates and the tension breaks with their simultaneous greeting:

"Hi."

"How're you?"

They fall back into silence, with their eyes fixed on the butcher's greasy hands as he inattentively handles cuts of meat, chunks of flesh slapping loudly against the marble, his knife slicing and the saw grunting against the bones.

The Basque man takes his meat and hands over the ledger where the butcher notes his expense. Then he says goodbye and leaves. The little old man in the beret steps forward and says something, then the door opens and Luisa appears:

"Good morning. Did you prepare my order?"

"Yes, miss, here it is."

"Thank you, goodbye."

"Bye."

Nefer thinks how easy it would be for the butcher to add extra monthly expenses to the Santa Clara ledger, as her mother is certain he does.

The other girl steps up to place her order and Nefer takes in her faded dress, her narrow back, and the messy braids crisscrossed at the nape of her neck. She thinks how they share a certain look, like little girls, that air of carelessness that Alcira and Doña María so often criticize her for. This thought floods her with a tide of anxiety as she remembers her secret. A sense of impotence rises to her throat, as if time has become something solid and she can almost hear its unstoppable current conspiring with her own body, which has betrayed her, tossing her to the mercy of the days. She grits her teeth and feels the blood drain from her face leaving her skin forgotten, stretched tautly over her bones. No, this can't be, it can't be real . . . Her senses retreat inward, toward the enemy lying in wait who she imagines like a pair of tireless eyes. It can't be . . . The butcher is talking to her:

"Are you feeling sick, Nefer?"

She jumps:

"Sick? No . . . Why do you say that . . .? I'm hot is all . . ." and she hastily hands him the bag and the ledger without knowing what she's doing or saying, "Short ribs please, or I'll take some skirt steak if that's all you've got, it's all the same . . ."

It's almost noon when she goes out. There's hardly any shade on the road. She unhitches the horse, places the bag atop the sheepskin, and jumps up.

This can't be real . . . It can't be happening . . . I have to go . . . but where? To . . . Yes. I have to go to . . .

She coaxes the horse into a gallop and passes, without noticing, a group of boys playing ball in the walled court, their shouts and whacks echoing after her.

The leaves of the trees and the wind pumps are motionless in the dense summer air; a muddy dog lying by the ditch looks up at her. The door to the chapel is closed.

Tomorrow . . . the mission . . . confession . . . Her heart clenches in fear. Someone who isn't her thinks inside of her: I have this afternoon to do it and I'm going to go . . . I don't know how . . . I have to wash the clothes and hang them out . . . I don't know how . . . but I'm going to go. . .

3

Nefer hears the creak of the bed as her mother falls onto it with a sigh and she pictures Don Pedro's small body rocked by the movement. She looks at Alcira sleeping unbuttoned and barefoot with an arm slung over her damp forehead; then she puts on her espadrilles and ties a kerchief under her chin. Blinded by the light outside, she squints and crosses the blazing patio.

She'd left the horse tied up on a long lead so he could graze in the shade of the trees, where almost all the birds are silent; the water she'd splashed onto his back is almost dry. Before mounting she gives him a pat.

"Poor old horse," she murmurs. "Poor old guy! You're really being put to work today, aren't you?"

She takes down the halter and bridles him, standing on tiptoe, but the horse draws his head back, tired of these monotonous motions.

She mounts and sets off at a walk, ducking and dodging the thorny branches of the hackberries. As they emerge from the trees the heat instantly envelops her, vibrating through the siesta hour and the wide yellow fields.

"Must be around two o'clock . . . I could be there by three . . ."

She kicks and takes off at a gallop, steering toward the thick grass that will absorb the footfalls. She doesn't want to think about the end of her journey, about the old lady she's never seen but with whom all her hope now lies. Her eyes pick out objects one at a time, attributing an exaggerated importance to each. Thistle, she thinks, thistle, partridge, dung, anthill, heat; and then she hears – one, two, three, four, one, two, three, four – as the hooves hit the ground. Slowly, sweat begins to appear behind the horse's ears and runs in dark strands down his neck where the reins chafe against his coat, churning up dirty foam. Little voices, little voices speak to Nefer, but she continues her journey, indifferent to them. Cow, she thinks, a Holstein, and another and another. That one's overheated. Lapwings. Two lapwings and their chick. Those piercing shrieks!

The road is a long dry tongue. Nefer watches her shadow galloping alongside her, she straightens up, shifts her arm, turns her head to see the changes in her silhouette. The sweat runs in stripes along the horse's haunches and down his legs; Nefer looks at the palm of her hand, dark dirt folded along each crease.

"Dapple horse," she says in a small voice, "you won't have to work tomorrow, okay? I'll sneak you some corn without them knowing. How does that sound? Tomorrow you can rest . . . Tomorrow the mission starts and . . ." She sharply redirects her thoughts, but the bitter taste lingers in her soul.

After walking through pastures and passing train tracks, meeting no other soul for more than an hour, the grass grows sparse on the ashy ground and the horse is blue with sweat. Nefer sees the little house appear in that translucent furnace of a day. Her heart shrinks.

Farther away, where the trees form a dark eyebrow, Don Pedro's sister lives with her family. But right now she isn't thinking about them, she's too preoccupied with this low house crammed up against the gigantic dried-out eucalyptus in the still air.

"Why did I come here?" She's overcome by an immense yearning for home. She's startled at the number of notions she's stored in her memory about the people she's going to see, this family with uncertain crisscrossing surnames, with an uncle who used to practice black magic and a witch doctor for a grandmother. Nefer tightens her grip on the damp reins and runs her tongue over her lips. Then she extinguishes her soul and continues along the road, which curves before reaching the house.

A buggy advances toward her, dark in the distance. Maybe they're going into town and the old lady will be there alone. That would make it easier. But what if it's the old lady in the cart? When she looks up, the buggy is in front of her and her heart skips a beat: her aunt and uncle pull on the reins and stop beside her.

"Nefer," says a voice that fills the air, "what are you doing in these parts?"

"You've come for a visit . . .? And just when we were leaving . . ."

"What a shame . . . but, why did you come all this way in this heat? Or has something happened?"

Nefer looks at the wheels of the cart and from somewhere inside she hears herself answer: "No . . . nothing has happened, nothing's wrong . . ."

"But, in this heat! Just look at the state your horse is in!"

Her aunt peers at her with two eyes that glimmer like ponds in her face. Her small frame is barely visible beside her husband's, which takes up almost the entire cart.

"And Pedro? How is he? Is he doing all right? And María? And the girls?"

"They're good, Auntie, everyone's fine, thanks."

Centuries of guile converge in Nefer and flow out to defend her words as the horse pants against her legs. Her uncle observes her from the shade of his hat and his teeth gleam beneath his mustache when he smiles.

"Fancy you coming all this way in this heat . . . Why didn't you wait for it to cool down? . . . Out here at siesta hour like some gringo. Or did you come to bring us some news?"

"No, Uncle, but I had work to do this morning and then if I'd have waited it would've been too late to get back. The patrona sent me to make sure everyone knew about the mission. It starts tomorrow."

"Uh-huh, we know, the patrona came herself to tell us the other day. What are you going to do now?"

"Well . . . I'll head on to the Borges house to give them the news, and then cool off a little before heading back."

Her aunt looks down at her hands, then says: "They know already. It's not worth your trouble to go over there."

"Well, that doesn't matter. I'll stop by and tell them anyway . . . I got my horse all tired out." She smiles.

"If you need to rest your horse you can go on up to the house, it's open."

"I'd better do my job, if not the patrona will be angry with me."

"How strange that she sent you even though she came herself. Do as you like, but don't dally. You know those people are no good."

"I know, I won't stay long. Bye."

"Bye."

She continues on her way and as she nears the house her horse's hooves thump against the parched ground. A dog comes out to bark, but the house appears to be sleeping with the roof pulled over its eyes. The dog barks and barks and finally decides to cautiously sniff the horse's legs. Nefer hesitates, then she claps her hands to let them know she's there but immediately regrets it and looks nervously around the dry yard smelling of scorched earth. Why did I come? She wipes sweat from her chin and leans down to look at her legs, which swing alongside the horse's belly.

Just then she turns her head and notices someone watching her from a distance. She sees a shirt, a beret, an arm resting on a fencepost, and a sense of unease slowly creeps up on her because she's recognized one of Old Lady Borges' grandsons. There are two of them and she's seen them many times, with their awkward posture, taking turns spitting words in high, catlike voices that make her feel uneasy. As though he were right in front of her, she can see his pale elfin face, his shifty eyes, and his hands fluttering like algae in a pond.

As she approaches the boy – she can't tell which one it is – she feels a great longing for the coolness of her room. She remembers one afternoon as a young girl when she and Alcira came to visit their aunt and uncle. There were the two Borges boys, crouched down, hugging their knees to their gaping mouths, and staring at them nonstop for an hour. Every once in a while, they whispered to each other or uttered a ripe swear word.

Trying to avoid his gaze, she greets him: "Afternoon . . ."

"Afternoon . . . What do you want?"

As he speaks he leans forward, slips some wire around a post, pulls it taut, and ties it with a skillful twist of his pliers, his colorless neck contorting beneath his bandana. Nefer's heart flip-flops as she notices his gaze fixed on her and not on his work. Pointing vaguely to the house, she stutters:

"Is anyone there?"

He turns back to his work and Nefer hears the snap of the wire. She sees hairs sticking out on his damp cheek and her heart pounds desperately. The silence drags on and he looks back at her with a wry smile. He says, his voice like a lapwing's: "Why? Are you looking for someone?" and his green eyes linger on her, full of pale, mocking glee.

The countryside staggers around Nefer, who grips the sheepskin in her hand and asks, trying to buy herself some time: "What. . . ?"

He leans over again laughing, then says: "You shouldn't be riding around on a horse, then . . . should you?"

Nefer's eyes see only a white sun spinning around and around filled with that voice, and barely breathing she mumbles: "What. . . ?" And she pretends to scratch her nose until the world settles.

"But actually," he says, "I guess you should be riding around on a horse, then . . . You need to gallop hard . . . right?"

With a high-pitched cackle he goes back to the wire, in his excitement his hands have gotten tangled up in it. Nefer can't think of an excuse to leave so she murmurs again: "Is anyone in there?"

"*Anyone, anyone,* who did you come to see? What *anyone*? If you came to see Granny, then say so. The witch is inside! If you came to see the other one, that one's over there, he's dying. If you care to know, if you want to see him. Ha! He's in the barn, with his feet in the air. Yeah! He's here too, if you want to see him. Or someone else? Just say it, say who!"

He takes a step back and trips over the spool of wire. Nefer watches him fall. Suddenly he's overcome with rage and beats at the ground with his fists, convulsing, then takes out his knife to stab the dirt one, two, three times before breaking into a yowl, his whole body shuddering.

A voice shouts from the house:

"Who's there?" And a woman in an apron appears in the doorway.

Nefer quickly pulls on the reins and moves toward the house, retreating from the shrieks that dissolve into a broken cackle, the voice repeating over and over:

"Gotta ride on horseback when you're a whore, when you're a whore, when you're a whore and a slut, on horseback, yeah."

The woman is large and her lurching voice is shrill as a clarion call.

"How are you, Nefer?" she greets her. "Hop down."

She dismounts, wondering how this lady can bear to live with sons like that, and when she ties up her horse in the shade she's filled with a sense of relief.

"How are things? Come on in."

"Goodandyou?"

The kitchen is small and dark. Nefer sees an old woman removing kernels of corn at the far end of the room.

"Good afternoon," Nefer mumbles.

"How are you? Have a seat."

"Okay."

She sits on a bench and the old lady continues her task using a method unknown to Nefer, scraping the corncobs against an iron rod placed across a box, producing a sawlike sound. The younger woman bends down and, trying not to wake the cat, picks up some twigs from under the stove and throws them onto the fire; she puts the kettle on and waits with her arms crossed. Nefer's eyes flash back to the pale face twisting and falling and the fists pounding in the dirt. A word she heard a long time ago forms on her lips: Cursed. He was born cursed. And the other one too.

Suddenly she remembers the story of a man whose roof was pelted with rocks day and night until he sent a message to the Borges uncle to say that if he kept on with his black magic he'd pay dearly for it. With that the stones stopped.

Startled, she notices the younger woman is standing in front of her.

"Would you like some?"

She accepts the mate and takes a sip as the two women talk to each other.

"Did he fall asleep?" the old lady whispers.

"Mmmm . . . I think so . . . At least he seems to have calmed down, I think."

"Who knows . . ."

Who's dying? Who's dying? Nefer wonders. She hands the mate back and answers their questions about her family, telling herself that if she doesn't speak up soon all will be lost. Anguish weighs upon her once again.

The younger woman goes to the door as if she's heard something. Nefer sees the lady's husband emerge from another part of the house with his hair sticking up, and out in the yard he puts his head under the stream of the water pump. Long siesta, she deduces.

Suddenly her blood freezes at the howling voice she had heard in the field, now very near but coming from the opposite direction to where the boy had stood. The women look at each other and the younger one rushes out.

The old lady murmurs:

"You see? He wasn't sleeping, poor thing . . ."

In the yard, the man has finished washing up and he looks toward the barn with wet hair dripping down his face. The voice whines: "No. No." Then it laughs hoarsely. Or cries, Nefer thinks. She hears the younger lady outside speaking in soothing tones.

Nefer watches closely as the old lady shakes her head: her arms and legs are scrawny and her deformed hands carelessly drop grains of corn. Shouldn't have come. Shouldn't have come. Shouldn't have come.

The large woman returns to the kitchen and the old lady asks: "How is he?"

"Says he doesn't want a compress, doesn't want anything. I don't know . . . His neck is all black . . ."

"We'll see . . ." She shakes her head gravely.

Cries that sound like the yelps of a dog filter in from outside. Someone asks Nefer a question, and she finds herself once again sharing the news about the mission. They're cursed. The brother tried to hang himself. That's what happened.

A log falls from the stove and breaks into glowing coals. Nefer tucks her feet back and the younger woman sweeps up the ashes. I'm going to get up and leave. After this mate. I'm going to get up and say goodbye.

She repeats this over and over in her mind until she suddenly finds herself standing and saying: "I'd better be getting back already."

"You're leaving . . . ? Now, in this heat . . . ?"

But they don't make much effort to stop her. She says goodbye to the old lady while the younger one walks her back outside into the daylight, which has become somewhat less oppressive. Far off, she sees the white shirt of the boy who's still repairing the wire fence gleaming in the sun.

When she reaches her horse someone calls out her name, and turning around, she sees the old lady in the kitchen doorway. She's taller than she'd looked and her dress hangs loosely from her straight shoulders.

"She's calling you," says the younger woman.

Nefer retraces her steps, walking back to the old lady, who has sparkling eyes and the teeth of a girl set into her muddy, waxen face.

"Ma'am?" she murmurs trembling.

The old lady's eyes are the only reality. Lowering her voice, she asks: "Is there anything else you want . . . ?"

Nefer clutches the fabric of her dress to keep from fainting into those eyes.

"What . . . ?" she asks.

"You don't want anything from me? You don't need anything? . . . Something . . ."

The entire world is concentrated in that face: the world with all its roads, trails, fields, furrows, rivers, and clouds.

"I . . ."

A current races through Nefer and before she can think how to answer she says: "Me, ma'am? . . . No . . . thank you . . . But no."

The old lady responds by looking off into the wide countryside: "Have it your way, then . . . Goodbye." And she goes inside.

Once Nefer is back on her horse, she almost feels like she's home.

4

Maybe it would be better to sit up, kick off the covers, lean against the rough wall, run her hand across her forehead, her damp hair, and close her eyes. The sounds mingling with the darkness are too intrusive: the heavy tick-tock of the alarm clock, Alcira's breathing, her parents snoring in the next room, the restless dogs in the night, the near and far-off roosters, her own heart pumping, rising to her throat, suffocating her. And on top of all this, time pacing ceaselessly past her bedroom door, tromping through the night, the world, carrying with it all things that will come to pass, things that will come to pass and cannot be stopped.

Nefer buries her face in her hands and it's as if she were peering into her nightmares. Her sister turns over in her sleep and the squeak of the cot startles Nefer; murmuring sounds percolate in her ears, throb in her head, converge in her heart to kick at her ribs.

She sits on the edge of the bed and her feet graze the rough bricks in search of her espadrilles. Outside, a dog lies heavily against the door, making it rattle. What time is it? She pulls a blanket from the bed, covers her shoulders, and walks toward the door with one arm outstretched.

It's not easy to get lost in this room with nothing more than an iron bed, a cot, and a table, but tonight fog swirls around her body and invades her mind. Her senses turn inward, refusing to guide her steps, which wander off. Nefer feels along the adobe wall but can't find the door. It has to be here, right here, four steps from the bed. Where is it? What room are we in? Isn't that Alcira breathing? Aren't those their alternating snores next door?

She traces the wall with her hand and a bit of loose plaster crumbles onto her feet. The dog scratches himself and rattles the door from somewhere unexpected. If the door is over there, that means she's been feeling along the wall where the calendar is hung. How did she get over here?

Holding onto the blanket with one hand, she stretches out the other and walks slowly through the room that has become an enemy hiding in the shadows, trying to disorient her with obstacles, erecting a wall in front of her face.

But this time, guided by the rattling sound, Nefer reaches the door. She gropes for the handle and feels the paint smooth and irregular on the wood, and the room takes shape again behind her. She bends down and silently lifts the bottom latch, then she pushes the door halfway open, pushes again, and goes out. The ticking clock, her fears, and the snoring all die out behind her, because on the patio there is only the night, its cold sweet smell filling the earth.

The dog licks her feet and jostles her blanket with the wag of his tail. Slowly, like a train passing in the distance, the wind pump lets out a long moan, and the crickets and frogs transform the air into an endless vibration.

In the star-laden night Nefer looks to the south, to the slightly darker bump where Santa Rosa's trees stand against the skyline, where the red light of the milking yard will shine out at three. But it's still too early. It might be midnight. Shivering, she steps off the path and walks over the packed earth of the yard to lean against a tree. Far away, the lapwings shriek with alarm.

She breathes deeply, and the fear that had been trapped under her skin by the darkness pours out through her eyes as they pick out objects in the distance, just as it flowed from her hands when they found the door, and as her fear is released the knot lodged in her throat loosens. How long until three o'clock? Here on her outpost they get up at four because the station is only three miles away, making it possible to get their milk to the train on time, but at Santa Rosa they start earlier because they're farther and have more cows.

So many months looking southward, she's almost forgotten that the landscape extends in other directions. Sometimes she sneaks out to wait for that instant when the light turns on like a red star, and although she can't see it, she knows exactly when Negro's brother is herding the cows through the empty field, the exact moment that Negro ties up the cows and starts to milk them, or loads the tanks onto the cart. She knows everything that's happening as if she too lived at Santa Rosa, between the adobe walls identical to her own, under the roof that Negro rethatched with new hay.

The dog licks her and the heat returns her thoughts to herself, and with her thoughts comes her distress. It's a weight too heavy to bear standing under this immense sky, and Nefer kneels down, pressing her face into the wooly fur of the dog, squeezing her eyes closed. She feels like she belongs to that fur, that heat, that smell, and not to the night with its vast scent of bitter grass from the plains and its mute dusting of stars.

When she closes her eyes it's as if she were opening them to her insides, to that spot where her misfortune grows and waits, and, clenching her teeth, she buries her face deeper into the dog's neck. But she doesn't cry. Disgraceful. I'm disgraceful. I'd be better off dead. Yes. Better off. I'd be better off if I died right now. Capitán. Capitán?

Capitán clumsily scratches himself and yawns with a small whimper, then she grabs him by two fistfuls of fur and shakes him until his teeth clatter. Capitán is her friend and he thinks she's playing, but no, she's shaking him in pure rage at the huge conspiracy closing in on her: misfortune conspiring with time, conspiring with her body, fearlessly united against her like a three-headed giant, and she's there all on her own.

"Capitán, you don't know anything and I don't know what to do. I thought maybe if I got on a horse and galloped fast enough, maybe if I worked hard enough, maybe if I slept deeply enough, when I woke up it would be gone . . . I thought if went to see that, that person, I could . . . if I went to see . . . Maybe if God helps me . . ." God? Maybe I should pray? If I say one Hail Mary and three Apostles' Creeds will a miracle occur? Maybe the Lord God is trying to scare me into praying more because I don't pray enough. But very few people pray a lot and disgrace like mine doesn't happen to any of them. Delia, for example, can't be that good, maybe God will punish her. Maybe her hair will get tangled in a tree and she'll spend days and nights there screaming till they find her, or the mare pulling her buggy will take off too fast and send her flying through the air right when Negro's looking. And I'll be there watching, and Negro and I will lock eyes and laugh together, and then we'll become friends, and at the dances I'll be the prettiest girl and he'll come straight over and ask me to dance, and she'll see us and die of jealousy, and she'll be forced to come to our wedding, and I'll be wearing a satin dress with a long train, and gloves, and then . . .

She turns her head and there's something hard caught in her throat, stifling her sobs, but still a long moan escapes her teeth and makes a muffled sound in the dog's fur.

5

When Nefer wakes up Alcira has just left the bedroom, allowing a sliver of cold night to slip in through the half-open door.

A rooster sings his strident scales, another imitates him, while another responds farther in the distance.

Today, she thinks, the mission.

Her face shows no expression but the air itself seems bitter. She works her feet into thick boots, pulls on a jacket, and steps out onto the patio, the sky heavy with stars. She automatically looks to the horizon where the little red light has come on; in the darkness she hears Juan's horse galloping back and forth as he herds the cows with shouts and whistles.

Nefer shivers and crosses her arms; through the kitchen door she can see Alcira in the dim candlelight using corncobs to start a fire and Don Pedro walks back from the trees buttoning his pants. From the corral comes the dry scrape of the branch and the twang of the wire as Juan closes the gate.

Nefer tiptoes past the room where her mother is sleeping, but stops when she hears her name.

"Nefer!"

She knows it would be wiser to pretend she didn't hear, but the voice calls out to her again, so she decides to respond: "What . . . ?"

"If I call you it's because I want you to come in!"

She pushes open the door and enters. The bed takes up half the room and a large mirrored wardrobe leans forward. A candle trembles on the bedside table illuminating Doña María's coarse hair. Her knees are like two multicolored hills under the quilt.

"What . . ."

"Come here."

She takes a step forward and stops at the foot of the bed. "What . . . ?"

"Come here, I said!"

Doña María leans forward, grabs her by the arm, and pulls her toward the bed. Her large hand lands on Nefer's face, back and forth, then she shakes her by the shoulders until her teeth rattle.

"What were you thinking?" she starts to say, chewing on her words, "What the hell were you thinking? Running around like some little hussy . . . like a piece of trash, taking off in the middle of siesta without telling anyone! . . . And . . . what for? . . . Why did you go over there? . . . Without asking for permission? . . . Why did you go? . . . Answer me, will you? How could you, without my permission! And don't tell me that tale about the mission . . . What do you think, that the patrona doesn't have any other messengers? . . . So she has to send you? Every other year she's managed to get the word out herself, but this time she decided to send you? . . . In the middle of siesta? Without telling anyone . . . just why would that be? Care to explain? Why? . . . Why? Speak up . . . Why?"

Nefer turns to stone, she speaks without moving her lips: "To let them know, that's why."

"To let them know! Oh really? Then let me call your aunt in here now, she's sleeping right next door. Let's call her in. The patrona herself drove over to let them know . . . But all of a sudden she had to send you too? All sneaky like . . . in the middle of siesta . . . What kind of messenger is that! Without telling anyone . . . Speak up! Or have you lost your tongue?"

"I went to let them know, the patrona told me . . ."

"To let them know! Is that it? To let them know? . . . In that heat? All alone, like some runaway, all the way over there . . . ?"

Don Pedro appears in the door. "It's late," he says. "We won't have the milk ready on time."

Doña María shouts: "Fine, take her! You can have her! The little hussy . . . You're going to answer me before the day's over . . . Go on! Go!"

Nefer steps past her father and goes out into the night. She walks to the corral where the lantern shines over a confusion of animals. She hobbles the first cow and begins to milk; behind her, Alcira sits at work yawning.

Nefer can't yawn. Her heart is twisted in knots.

To keep from crying she says to herself: I knew it, so why am I so upset? I knew this was going to happen.

She becomes immersed in the dirty sweet smell of her work, the heat of the cow, and the dull sound of the alternating streams of milk hitting the bucket. Why am I so upset? I knew this would happen. . . A drop of milk hits her; she unties the cow and goes to the next one.

I wish all the cows were like Princesa and I didn't have to tie them up . . . She winds the rope around the cow's legs, but the animal is nervous and kicks to avoid being hobbled.

"Hey! Be still."

She reties the knots and gets to work, but the cow moves and kicks until one leg comes loose and knocks over the bucket full of milk.

Nefer looks at the big white stain being sucked up by the ground, she lets herself fall back on her heels, buries her fists in her eyes and sobs. The pain moves up her throat slowly, stabbing like knives. It's as if each sob were a tiny baby being born, but her wails are lost to the mooing and stamping of the cows. She's covered by a veil of tears that erases the world and soaks her face, her hands, and the sleeves she hides behind.

A voice rises up from the din of indifferent sounds, and through the blur of her tears she sees two large muddy boots beside her, work pants and two buckets hanging from two dirty hands.

Juan speaks to her again, his faded beret pulled down to his eyebrows.

"Nefer."

She doesn't know how to respond. She looks up at him as she wipes her face with her sleeve.

"Hey," he says, setting down a bucket and scratching his head. "If there's something wrong you can count on me . . . If you need anything . . ."

"No. No . . ."

She's flooded by a new river of tears. Juan sets down the other bucket and fumbles in his pocket for a wrinkled handkerchief. He leans down and presses it into her hand.

"All right then," he says. "Bye."

He picks up the buckets and walks away.

Nefer buries her face in the handkerchief and wails.

Negro, she thinks. Negro.

Then she turns the bucket back upright, grips it tightly between her knees, and milks. When she looks up, the stars have changed position and Nefer is the center of that sky. It circles around her like a massive gleaming ship, as much a victim to the whims of time as she is, equally submissive to the shifting of the hours, and in her anguish she clenches her fists, soiled with mud and milk.

6

Riding in a wagon is like skimming over the surface of the earth, viewing the countryside from above while the planks jostle nosily below. Doña María's face is white from so much rice powder. She sits composed with her feet tucked under the seat the way she does at dances, her best manners on display.

Nearing the chapel, at the edge of town, there are buggies and automobiles and tiny people walking by.

"Are we running late?" says Doña María.

"There seem to be a lot of people."

"The priest will be glad . . ."

"There are the folks who work La Florida Ranch . . ."

"And here come the patrones in their motorcar..."

A plume of dust rises from the plains, trailing a car that looks like a toy in the sudden gleam of sunlight.

Don Pedro holds the reins in lifeless hands. He's wearing a clean handkerchief with the two ends tied in a knot at his neck; he sees an owl in the path as he rides past and thinks it looks just like María, but his face remains wooden, unaltered by laughter or sorrow.

Sitting beside him is Alcira, the prettiest girl in town. Her arms are three times the size of Nefer's. Don Pedro admires her like a flower out in the meadow: lovely, a beauty to behold; she won't be an easy catch.

The wagon needs to be overhauled because parts are coming loose and heaven forbid an accident should occur. The ironwork and the wooden planks clank loudly.

"And that motorcar, over there?"

"Hmmm..."

"They must be guests at El Destino Ranch."

"Or they've bought a new car..."

Nefer is not looking. Since they arrived, since they made their way around the bend and into town, her attention has been somewhere else.

Her eyes are on the general store, on the hitching post where the horses are tied up between buggies. She's too far away to be able to tell the horses apart and so, raising her arms and pretending to adjust her headscarf, she shifts her eyes to the right, quickly, beyond the pasture and into the horizon, in case a certain horseman were to approach, dark in the distance but recognizable by his posture, by the curve of his arm, or by the gait of his horse.

But the countryside is deserted and silent under the sun.

Nefer doesn't know how to get rid of this fear that gnaws at her stomach and haunts her dreams. Last year she was scared of confession, but that was different. And this chapel, where every step echoes and echoes and where every gesture is caught by watchful eyes – what a shabby suit! What a long confession! What a face lined with sin! And the priest there listening, inside, in that cage of his. He might tell Doña María, Don Pedro, or maybe even the rich folks from the ranch in the middle of their lunch, and then she'd be the talk of the town.

She used to like the mission. They'd have stories to tell for months afterward, but today Nefer would rather dig a hole in the ground, even if it meant digging with her own hands until her fingernails bled, she would dig with her raw fingers until her nails broke off, then with her arms when her fingers wore down, and inside that deep hole she would bury herself, close her eyes and cover them with dirt and slowly turn into roots or grass or mud, without dreams, alone, her fears forgotten. Because the days are yoked together, one starts and another is inevitably on the way, and then another, and another, and they must be endured. Because man is a pathetic creature, he cannot raise his knife and say, "I can no longer endure this" without saying, "I can no longer endure myself." He will solve nothing by sticking the knife into his belly. Because the days come and go like an endless herd tromping through an open gate.

Nefer runs her hand along a rough plank, back and forth, back and forth, back and forth. Planks are serious, there's a kind of virtue about them. But the wagon is a rickety bag of bones; it jumps, creaks, rattles. Junk heap of a vehicle. The countryside spins as they jostle along.

What if . . . what if someone were to come now and tell them: the priest got sick, he had to go back to the city, there is no mission.

There's no mission, no need to greet everyone, no people to look you up and down and say: you're so thin, so pale. What if there's none of that?

Of course there's a mission. The town is filled with people, and yet so empty. All those horses tied up but there's no one around. Could he have a new horse? Nefer knows what his tack looks like, and Negro – no, Negro's isn't there.

The horses pulling the wagon know the way by heart, they turn and stop at the hitching post.

"Good morning, Doña María . . ."

"Good morning. How d'you do? Good morning, ma'am . . ."

"Nice weather . . ."

"Morning. My how the boy's grown!"

"Are we on time . . . ?"

" . . . young priest . . ."

" . . . yes, let's go in . . ."

It's a box, a little box inside this large building, and the wood creaks, it creaks. The legs of the girl kneeling inside stick out; when she gets up it will be Nefer's turn. Her turn, her turn, Nefer's turn; a boy comes to light the candles, he stands on his tiptoes holding out a pole: the flame flickers, rises, stretches, no, the candle is stubborn. Again, the flame flickers, it gets bigger, he moves away. Two flames, another candle.

The heads all in a row donning colorful kerchiefs, Raquel's with a blue boat on it and another with lettering – who knows what it says – red flowers, stars.

The wood creaks, her heart jumps. Is it her turn? No. How did it go last year? What did the priest ask? She can't remember, he was a little old man, he was nice. Has Negro arrived yet? She doesn't dare turn around, so many sounds, footsteps, maybe his, maybe . . .

What if she leaves? What if she doesn't confess? Says she feels bad, like Alcira did last year? She's so frightened by this chapel where every footstep says: here I am, stepping forward. Look, I'm on the left, I'm getting closer to the confessional, I'm kneeling down, pay attention please. The people pay attention. When the confessional finally creaks open they watch to see the look on each person's face; full of penance? Full of sin? The face says nothing, sometimes it even smiles a little, hiding something. But, what happens before that? The priest always asks a question. What does he say? What does he say?

One's soul must be clean for communion; otherwise hell itself will slip inside, the demons will come, and if you suffer an accident and die you'll burn for all eternity.

She won't confess. But the girl before her gets up, her turn has come. Kneel down, little wooden grate so close to her face, fog inside her head. Oh, there's a voice. It's saying something, what?

" . . . Forgive me Father, for I have sinned . . ." it says.

"Forgive me Father, for I have sinned," Nefer repeats, hoarsely.

"How long since your last confession?"

"It . . . um, it's been a year . . ."

"What sins do you remember, my child . . . ?"

"Um . . . I . . . I told some lies and . . . and, um, what's it called? I told lies . . . and . . ."

Nefer finds herself surrounded by night, all at once specks of light glimmer loudly. She answers in monosyllables: yes, no. She understands very little, hears words she doesn't know, answers only with short words: yes, no.

The priest says: purity, and by the tone of his voice it seems like he knows. "You haven't sinned against purity?" She doesn't know. Did she? But, what if she didn't? She says: "I don't know." The little voice clarifies: "You haven't had any wicked thoughts? Wicked desires . . . ?" Oh, wicked thoughts, wicked desires, when she dreamed of revenge, when she wanted Delia to drown in a ditch, yes, she's had them, "Yes, Father."

"And nothing else? Wicked actions . . ."

No, she hadn't acted on them, she'd only wished for them, but she'd done something else, once, she, she . . . She no longer knows what she's saying. The priest is asking things but Nefer can only hear her heart pounding, which brings her back to the single reality of the moment. She rushes to fill the silence.

"What?" she asks.

"All right . . . Now the Act of . . ."

The act of what? "Yes, Father," she says. What is it? She decides to stay quiet. The priest begins: "O my God, I am heartily sorry . . . !" Oh, she knows the Act of Contrition, she learned it. She mumbles it slowly to conceal wayward words, but is the priest talking to her? "What are you saying, Father?" Oh, no! He's praying. She continues: "And I . . . firmly . . . resolve . . ."

"All right," says the priest, "go in peace and may the Lord bless you."

Go? How? What about what she was going to say? What was she going to say?

"Father . . ." But there's no one there, another man has knelt down and the priest is listening to his confession. She gets up and the church spins. Has Negro arrived? She goes back to her pew and closes her eyes. At least she can close her eyes at church. A slow horde of steps comes shuffling in, the folks from Santa Clara, Doña Dolores with her daughters Doña Mercedes and little Susana, and behind them Luisa with a thick book like Nefer would like to have. They sit down in the front row.

Of everyone inside the chapel very few would think of making their way down to the front without dying of embarrassment.

Except for Delia, thinks Nefer, and as she thinks this she hears the clicking of heels and sees Delia approaching the altar rail, where she sets down a bouquet of flowers and walks slowly back to her seat, pursing her lips. Nefer lowers her eyelids and is flooded by a wave of hatred. To think that Negro might be watching her . . .

But Negro is leaning against the back wall watching how glints of light reflect off the priest's glasses from time to time. He takes a step to the left and it's time for the Gospel. The church echoes with the sounds of people getting up, pushing back the pews, coughing, and sneezing.

Nefer dares to turn her head and discovers Negro leaning against the back wall with two other men; when she turns her head toward the altar again her neck feels like stone and her heart pounds in her throat.

Doña Mercedes takes her seat as the Gospel is ending. She always anticipates the movements of the ritual with a grave expression, setting an example for the ignorant masses, indicating which behavior to follow, and a dark satisfaction rises up in her when she hears from behind the buzz sparked by her action, like the slight delay of a mantle trailing the steps of a king. It's as if she were somehow a second priestess dictating the movements of the faithful through her gestures.

The priest finishes the Gospel and Nefer watches him lift his hands from the altar, stand before the crowd, and fix his eyes on the door leading out to the brilliant morning and the general store across the way. He raises his hand and slowly makes the sign of the cross.

The church sounds like a dovecote: several children run from pew to pew, one cries and another coughs. The priest opens his mouth but the first few words are drowned out by the trumpeting of a man blowing his nose, then feigning a cough before sliding his hands back into his cuffs.

"Beloved brethren, today's Gospel, on the fifth Sunday of Advent, is a clear lesson on what faith represents before the eyes of God. Faith, a theological virtue, essential for the life of the soul . . ."

The life of the soul, thinks Negro. How did it go . . .? The soul of . . . Oh, right, "from the soul." How pretty! And how sweetly Julia danced! It's hard to believe what a fine musician that gringo José is, when he plays the waltz it sounds as good as it does on the radio . . . This priest, how does he manage to wear all those layers of clothes and the little green poncho on top? Does he bring it all with him in a suitcase or do they keep it here at church for him?

"Because if we don't have charity – if we don't make room in our hearts for charity, my dear brothers, how can we aspire to attain the eternal reward?"

Nefer bends down to scratch her foot. She knows that her family members, like herself, slip into oblivion during the sermon, between unfamiliar or commonplace words, thinking they've gotten the gist until they ultimately become entirely absorbed by their own affairs.

"Charity is love . . ."

A long howl echoes across the church and a woman pulls her son into her arms and shakes him to quiet him down. The priest from last year had said in such cases: "Ma'am, please take the boy outside for a moment until he has calmed down so we can finish . . ." but this priest just coughs again and continues, raising his voice:

"It is our love, my brothers, for the soul of God, and our fellow man's love for the soul of God. One cannot love God without loving one's fellow man. As we do unto ourselves, says Jesus. But it is more than unto ourselves, for as He says: what better proof of love than to lay down one's life for one's friends?"

Nefer imagines Negro in great danger, then she arrives on the scene, risking her life, jumping in to save him, and Negro smiles gratefully and finally speaks to her.

"He loved us like this, did he not? He became obedient to the point of death, says Saint Paul, *even death on a cross.* Do you need any greater proof of love, my brethren? We must model ourselves after Him ..."

The priest stops, takes his handkerchief from his sleeve and blows his nose. Negro thinks he would lose anything he tried to keep tucked into a sleeve like that.

"There is another teaching from today's Gospel we must take as a lesson, my brothers, and that is trust in God. Trust, dear brothers, trust. Which of us, in a moment of pain or anguish, would not call upon our own mother, our own father, to ask for help? Father of mine, Papá, this is happening to me, I'm having this problem. Mother of mine, Mamita, help me with this – who would not? And well, dear brethren, God is father and mother of all mankind, for being the Creator is more than being a parent, it's more than ..."

Don Pedro listens gravely, sitting uncomfortably at one end of the pew, and although there's easily enough room at the other end for at least four men to sit, he must stay where he is because after all the effort of getting to church in the first place he doesn't have the energy to make another decision. He can feel his feet tight in his boots and he'd like things to wrap up so that on his way out he can ask the other men's opinions about old Hernandez's cattle, but he listens with the vague notion that merely taking in all this momentous language he doesn't understand will somehow dignify him.

"Today is the first day of the mission, the first of these days during which — thanks to the generosity of several kind souls from this fine town — it is possible for you to fulfill the precepts of Our Holy Mother the Church, as prescribed by God. I would advise you to take advantage of these limited days: to baptize your children, confess, receive communion . . . Marriages that need to be recognized will be certified, and so on . . . Let us take advantage of these days, my brothers, let us not be ungrateful to God, to whom we owe so much. I will now repeat the schedule. Communion Mass will be at eight o'clock. As you all know, in years past there were two Masses, but this year I was forced to travel alone because the priest who was meant to come with me fell ill. Catechism for children will be at four o'clock; the blessing of rosaries will be at six o'clock. . ."

Nefer imitates the movements of the people sitting in the front rows, and once the Apostles' Creed has ended she sits back down. She notices that her mother has followed Doña Mercedes's example, fanning herself with a holy card she removed from the missal. Now a strange high-pitched sound rises, its wavering notes joining and stretching on sourly, and the music fills the chapel.

The station master's wife studied piano, and therefore she is in charge of all musical performances. The most serious pieces in her repertoire are the *Ave Maria*, the *Salve Regina*, and an aria from an operetta which is reserved for the moment of Consecration.

Nefer thinks that if she were in charge of music perhaps Negro would fall in love with her and they would end up getting married, but she knows that she's no good at studying. She looks sidelong at Delia, who pivots in her high heels, one foot balancing on the tip of the heel. She finds the gesture admirable and looks away. She's filled with a dark sadness and thinks: why me, and not someone else? These things have to happen to somebody, but why me?

She looks down at her body showing no signs.

What about Communion? She's still riddled with sin because the priest didn't hear about it, so if she takes Communion she'll be flooded with demons and then she'll be like the Borges family, cursed.

The air inside the chapel tenses up, pulsating and throbbing with an ominous presence and the very act of breathing feels bold, as if all events until now were leading up to Communion. Doña Mercedes is the first to line up, and Nefer closes her eyes to avoid meeting her mother's gaze, which will command her to stand up and follow along.

Nefer doesn't register the exact moment it occurs, but she knows that now, without any signal from the priest, people have started to approach the altar.

Once the music ends she clasps her hands together, but then hears the tromping of boots hastily approaching the choir, followed by whispering. She'd like to take a look, as the boy sitting in front of her does, but she doesn't dare turn around. The only sounds in the chapel are the murmurs of the priest and the rustling of some pigeons who have made their nest above the window.

Suddenly, without any warning, one sustained note thunders through the room, vibrating and pressing in at the walls. There is a split second of unease among the congregation, which quickly transforms into grave admiration. Nefer realizes that the sound of the boots had come from Mr. Constanzo Baris, who arrived late. He is the owner of the dulce de leche factory and has a singing voice like those you might hear on the radio. He sings in the factory or at the train station, walking back and forth on the platform, and often gives performances inside the chapel. He has unfortunately never learned the repertoire favored by the station master's wife so for those songs Mr. Constanzo can only keep time with a tapping foot.

That man has more millions of pesos than hairs on his head, Doña María has been known to say, and those around her will nod their heads in agreement.

Pews scrape the floor as people get to their feet and begin to exit in a disorderly stream. As they reach the door, voices burst into greetings that intermingle and echo back into the church, sweeping aside the becalmed atmosphere of prayer.

Nefer would like to stay in her pew with her eyes closed until there was no one left outside but she doesn't dare, so she marches slowly to the door, the boy behind her treading on her heels with every step. Her mother might scold her for not having received Communion.

Doña Mercedes's voice chimes loudly from outside:

"Yes, Catechism for children at four o'clock, blessing with the Eucharist at five . . . Good day! How are you, dear? My, how you've grown! Hello Juana! What did you think of the sermon? . . . Did you enjoy it? . . . Ah, is this the little one getting baptized? . . . What a gorgeous pair of eyes!"

The voices rise, come together, and surge, pierced by sharp laughter.

There goes the patrona of El Destino Ranch, walking back toward the automobiles like a sluggish black flagpole through the shiny morning, exchanging hellos.

The men have already started walking over to the general store, except for the older ones, who are waiting to exchange greetings near the church.

Nefer sees that Negro is crossing the road, she sees him from behind dressed in gray, his knife, his chambergo hat, and the world blurs all around him. A voice, which for an instant she fears might be her own, calls out to him:

"Negro! Negro Ramos!" And it causes him to stop in the middle of the road marked by wagon tracks, and his head turns.

It's one of the ladies, the patrona of San Gervasio Ranch, calling out to him. Negro retraces his steps, moving closer. Nefer feels her legs buckle, become limp.

"Ma'am?" he says, taking off his hat.

"How d'you do?" The woman holds out her hand.

"How d'you do, ma'am," he touches it in the fleeting suggestion of a handshake.

Don Pedro always talks about a rodeo at San Gervasio where he teamed up in cattle cutting with this same woman some thirty years before. A handsome woman, he always said, she'd make a good wife for a poor man. But no poor man would allow his wife such fancies, and anyway that time has passed, the woman still rides but no longer indulges in such games.

"You're working at the milking yard now?"

"At the milking yard, uh-huh, yes ma'am."

Someone grabs Nefer by the arm, making her turn:

"Here's my goddaughter," a voice says.

Her family is standing around Doña Mercedes.

"I keep telling her she needs to put on some weight."

"Yes ma'am, I know. But! . . . She doesn't eat a thing! . . . She's entirely lost her appetite . . . I'd like to teach her a lesson . . ."

"One has to eat . . ."

Nefer doesn't have eyes for these people. She doesn't have ears for these words. Words made of manure, that's what they are. Words made of nothing.

By the time she's able to get away, the conversation between Negro and the other woman is coming to an end.

" . . . I have some foals there, and since Francisco's fallen ill . . ."

"Yes, ma'am, of course. In the afternoon, more than likely, I'll be on over."

Negro says goodbye and the lady says in a dry voice:

"All right! Everyone from San Gervasio, we're leaving. Carlitos, go on over to the general store and let everyone from the ranch know that we're leaving now."

The farewells hasten and Doña Mercedes raises her voice:

"Tomorrow, eight o'clock Mass. Today, Catechism at four . . . Oh, Father, come have breakfast with us . . . Let me introduce you to . . ."

Across the road some of the families are climbing into the buggies and departing; everywhere the sounds of wood, ironwork, and whips, while the automobiles start up their engines and the horsemen ride off.

Nefer walks away from the hubbub and looks over at the general store. She sees Negro who, with a cigarette in his mouth, unties his horse, laying his hand on the withers and his foot in the stirrup. He mounts as lightly as a bird as he tightens his grip on the reins to control the nervous animal, who's already almost at a trot, kicking up a small cloud of dust until he reaches the curve in the road, where he turns.

Nefer lowers her eyes like someone closing a reliquary and replays him in her mind walking away over the tracks, then turning back to respond to the lady's call, chatting with one foot crossed in front of the other, the toe of his boot rocking in the dirt as he scratches his neck, pointing to the horse as his white teeth smile from under his little mustache.

Her mother is calling her. Anguish once again floods her limbs, and she drags her feet back to the wagon.

7

In the kitchen darkened by the storm Nefer hands a gourd of mate to her father, and he sets down the reins he's been oiling to take a sip. No one pays attention to the car race on the radio – not Doña María sewing by the door, not Alcira who yawns keeping watch on a frying pan, not Capitán who trembles from time to time.

Rain streams in from the corner of the roof and drips slowly down the side of the cupboard.

Nefer sighs; her limbs feel thick and tired.

Like mud in my veins, she thinks.

"Are you finished using the table?" she asks her sister.

"Yes."

"Well then clean up already, I have to iron."

A clap of thunder echoes through the sky, it fills the air and now the rain closes in, falling more intensely. The tinny strumming of Juan's guitar twangs faintly through the downpour.

"My oh my," says Doña María. "I don't think Juan is getting any better at the guitar."

"Sure he is, a little. It's just that he's a slow learner, but he's getting there."

Nefer doesn't think Juan will ever learn to play well, but she envies him all alone in his room, focused on his task. She'd like to be able to get away from her mother's surliness, from Alcira's indifference, and the radio – to escape from everything, lock herself away, close her eyes and think about Negro's smile, his voice saying hello, how he hops on his horse, and how he dismounts to smoke a cigarette squinting his eyes, but instead she's dejected by the room shrouded by rain.

Doña María looks at her:

"And you, why haven't you started your ironing? Are you going to wait until it's time to eat before you use the table?"

"But – didn't I just tell her to clean up already? It's covered in flour, what am I supposed to do?"

"C'mon lazybones! And you too, you and your buñuelos. Wipe down the table, would you?"

Alcira grabs a rag and wipes the table off, then she looks at her sister.

"Are you happy now? . . . What a fuss . . . You could've started heating up the iron in the meantime."

She walks back to the stove and drops little balls of dough into the oil, which crackle and pop over the flame. The smell of fried food impregnates the kitchen and Nefer feels revulsion rising inside her. Holding her breath, she places some coals inside the box iron, and while she waits for it to heat up she leans against the open door and looks out at the horizon blurred by water, at the vast misty countryside. The gulps of fresh air clear her head and the dampness makes her loose wisps of hair frizz. The dapple horse must be all blue with water, the poor thing; she almost smiles. Princesa too, and the grass will be fresh and moist when they eat . . . Her hooves won't hurt the next time she gallops.

"Move over. You're blocking my light," her mother says.

Nefer doesn't want to inhale the smell of the kitchen, and as she moves back inside she tries to think about something else.

First the shirt, then Juan's handkerchief, my blouse . . .

She covers the table with a blanket and presses the iron into the shirt. The wrinkles start to fade after several heavy passes.

Alcira tries a buñuelo, chewing thoughtfully.

"Tastes funny," she says, "Do you want to try one Mamá?"

"Let's see . . ." Doña María stabs one and eats it. "Tastes just fine to me . . . Really, it's just fine. What's funny about it? Gimme another."

"There's something odd about the taste . . . Not bad, just different . . . what could it be?"

Don Pedro approaches and she holds out the plate and fork to him, which he takes and tastes with careful consideration.

"Tastes good," he murmurs, and smiles with his vague expression of gentle teasing. "I think it's good, it's . . ."

"Here, try one," Alcira says to her sister.

"No thanks, I'm not hungry . . ."

"C'mon try one . . . So you can see what I mean. . ."

"No, leave me alone, I'm not hungry . . ."

Nefer leans over and blows on the embers inside the iron. Her mother turns and looks at her:

"Like a little bird, this one is: 'I don't want any, I'm not hungry, I don't want to.' Just look at her. Miserable! A face like death, even the patrona said something to me yesterday . . . This can't go on . . . You're going to start eating this very instant, and I don't want to hear any anything else about it . . . Go on, give her a buñuelo."

The rain gushes down from the edge of the straw roof and another clap of thunder splits the sky and then fades into dull echoes. The radio roars with engines and shouts from the broadcaster announcing the race: *Number nine, number nine, attention! He's about to pass! . . . We're letting our listeners know that number nine is passing . . .*

Nefer shakes her head:

"I don't want one . . ."

"Enough already with the 'I don't want one!' Today it's the buñuelos, tomorrow potatoes, yesterday it was the meat, and day after day — you're pure skin and bones. That's it! That's enough already! Today we're starting over. C'mon, eat one! . . . As finicky as a pregnant lady . . . I don't need this! . . . Eat up . . . Just one!"

Nefer's hands clutch at the shirt she's ironing and she crumples it up into a ball:

"I don't want to! I said I didn't want any! I don't want any because I'm going to throw up! Because I'm going to have a baby! I *am* pregnant . . . All right? And you could have figured it out, since you know so much . . . Or didn't you realize? Didn't you notice that my stomach is growing? Are you blind, is that it? . . . Are you stupid, is that it?"

She runs out into the rain, stumbling over everything, tearing through the morning and the puddles. There, beyond the tree line amongst the branches, she embraces a tree and lets herself fall. She bites her fist and moans, her face clinging to the bark like wet velvet. She moans and howls as if ripping the skin off her bones, as if her soul could somehow be released through her voice and free her from disgrace. She claws at the tree trunk and peels off pieces of moss that smell of rain.

Good . . . good, good! It's better that they know. Now they know, let them deal with it, let them be ashamed, let them deal with it, let them die, let them die, let them die.

She bites her fist and sobs. Then she grabs the branches with both hands and shakes them until a glistening downpour showers her shoulders and dampens her hair and skin, which quivers under the brilliant drops of water. Her dress sticks to her body and she stretches out her arms, clutches the branches, and shakes them until not a drop of water remains.

The chill calms her and she considers going back.

All right. What do I care? What do I care.

She walks along the damp path, the doves fluttering up with every step as they noisily abandon their nests. But when she sees Doña María's silhouette watching from the doorway she switches directions and decides to seek refuge in the barn.

The dog has seen her and runs toward her affectionately.

In the dark barn Nefer sits on the shaft of the buggy. Doña María appears at the door.

"Are you there?"

She doesn't answer. Her mother enters and as her eyes get used to the light she sees Nefer motionless beside the dog.

"Why won't you answer me? Is it true what you said? Answer me, will you? Tell me if what you said is true."

"And why wouldn't it be true?"

Her mother approaches:

"Are you crazy?" she yells. "Are you nuts?"

Nefer stands and yells even louder:

"No! I'm not crazy! I already told you what I am! Didn't you understand? Do you want to hear me say it again? I'm . . ."

She doesn't have time to finish: her mother raises an arm and her hand falls on Nefer. She covers her head. I wish I could die. I wish I'd never been born . . . she thinks. Her mother yells enraged:

"Whose is it?"

She wants to say: it's Negro's, because it *is* Negro's, it's his, but she doesn't say anything. She thinks: maybe I'll die.

Doña María straightens her up by the shoulders and shakes her:

"What have you done, you little hussy! When? Where?"

The nape of her neck prickles from the onslaught, the fog. She closes her eyes and thinks: Maybe the roof of the barn will cave in and crush us and it will all be over.

8

She stays in the barn and her eyes sweep across the shadows of the farm instruments and hanging tools. She imagines they must be finishing lunch in the kitchen, but after her mother bemoaned her fate, cursing God, she heard no further signs from outside.

An intermittent dripping lingers from the rain, and out of nowhere a rooster crows.

She decides it's time to go back inside. Too bad it's cool out today and nobody's going to take siesta.

She sulks into the bedroom where Alcira is sewing and lies down on the cot, covering her face with a pillow.

A wasp buzzes and buzzes and the silence begins to quaver. Nefer thinks if she could just slow her breath down she might end up falling asleep, but when she closes her eyes all she can see is her mother's arm coming down, her mother's mouth spitting threats. Alcira speaks and her voice rings loud and clear:

"Why did you lie today?"

Nefer decides to pretend she's asleep but Alcira's voice sounds so sure she's awake that she can't do it. Without opening her eyes she responds:

"I didn't lie."

In the silence that follows she squints her eyes open to see her sister's expression. Alcira is hunched over her work.

The wasp buzzes and vibrates against the ceiling. Maybe I'll fall asleep, Nefer thinks.

Alcira speaks again, with a slight hesitation:

"When . . . did it happen?"

Nefer pauses.

"A while back."

Alcira jabs the needle in, puts down her work, and stares at her hand.

Then she asks:

"Did it . . . did it hurt?"

Nefer presses her lips together and suddenly an inkling of superiority sweeps over her, a sorrowful glory. She doesn't respond.

Knowing that her sister feels humiliated by her silence, she relishes the revenge with a smug smile. Then she peeks out from the pillow. Alcira has taken her sewing back up, but she soon speaks again:

"And now what . . . ?"

A chill of helplessness runs through her. She'd like to share her dread with Alcira, sob over her abandonment, ask why these things happen to certain people, but she says:

"What do you care?"

She regrets it immediately and wants to say something else. But Alcira just shrugs and silence once again blankets the room as the desperate hum of the wasp in search of sunlight reaches a crescendo.

9

Standing next to the gate they wait for the bus to appear at the end of the road. Doña María sighs and Nefer knows the sigh means that it's getting hot and everything is weighing on her: the heat, the day in the city wearing those shoes, and a daughter like this.

Nothing matters anymore. Not the sun, not the doctor, not her furious mother. Nefer has ears and therefore she can hear, and a mouth she uses to eat, but the world swirls around her like rushing water, and she is solemn and nothing matters. In time her body will start to swell, and later still it will shrink again, it doesn't matter, it doesn't matter anymore, everything is born and then dies, but nothing matters.

The bus becomes visible near the chapel, kicking up dust as it nears.

It looks like the refrigerator from the ranch, thinks Nefer, but on wheels.

"Oh! Here it comes!" her mother exclaims after a while. "I'm so embarrassed to show my face on the bus."

Nefer shrugs because Doña María knows that nobody else is aware of her predicament, but when the bus pulls up they both feel somewhat intimidated. The mother hoists herself up with difficulty, Nefer follows behind, and out of the corner of her eye the coach seems to be filled with wide-brimmed chambergos.

They say hello and sit down. Doña María converses with the woman sitting in front of them, with the one behind, and with a girl who's carrying a boy on her lap. She asks after their families and nods at their answers. Nefer scans the other passengers and notices that what seemed like countless hats were just three: two worn by men in the front seat and another in the back.

They wear big felt chambergos, like Negro. But these men are fat and red-faced and come from far and wide, and Negro's poncho is more handsome than that one ...

The men talk cattle and laugh, and Nefer looks at them in the reflection of the driver's rearview mirror, the folds of their boots like small accordions. Why can't Doña María just take her word for it? She's not some young fool, and three months is three months, and she's been feeling awful, and all the vomiting . . . What's the point of going to the doctor, making such a fuss, spending money?

She thinks of the way Alcira looked at her, with unexpected respect or a glint of scornful compassion. And everyone getting worked up and treating her differently, except for her father who just kept braiding leather, sipping mate, and watching the horses. Thinking of him is like dimming the lights, pulling the sheets over her head, and finally feeling at peace.

In the distance, two people are waiting in the road and the conversations pause until the coach stops and they get on, greet the others, and take their seats.

The view from the window unfolds all the way to the green horizon.

Perhaps telling the doctor will serve to purge the sin from inside. But no. A doctor is not the same as a priest. The things that get into her head!

In the mirror, Nefer looks at the legs of the fat man discussing his cattle. She notices the silver flower on his belt, peeking out from under his sweater. Negro's belt has his initials trimmed in gold and is hung with shiny coins. Few are as beautiful. When Nefer was a little girl she wanted to be a man, to be able to flaunt such glittering finery at parties.

The bus slows down and honks its horn, making way through a herd of cattle. The cowhands whistle and gallop among the cows. As the bus passes, everyone simultaneously turns their heads to identify the cattlemen. Then they begin to comment and estimate prices, origin, and buyer.

The woman in the seat behind them talks to Doña María about Alcira:

"Most importantly," she says, "like I always say, she's a pretty girl who hasn't gotten too proud or rude as a result . . ."

Doña María lowers her eyes modestly:

"Well, ma'am," she says fidgeting, "for me the most important thing is that she's well-behaved . . ."

Nefer looks at the fields and the dark trees and hopes that her mother's shoes hurt her feet today.

A car honks at the bus and passes them.

"From Santa Clara," someone says.

"Hmmm. Is that Luisa with her aunt?"

"There were three people . . ."

"They must be going shopping . . ."

They begin to pass houses and gardens, the sides of the road adorned with sad palm trees. Once they reach downtown the passengers begin to gather their belongings and the women comb their hair. The last stop is outside the hotel.

The sun beats down on the streets and the sidewalks burn. Walk, walk with a piece of paper in hand asking which way, how many blocks, as the numbers get closer each one is like sip of fresh water, and when at last the green door and the bronze plaque appear, she can't help but feel like the whole thing is unreal.

A dark girl with an apron opens the door, and when they walk into the office several people turn to look.

Maybe they think Mamá is the sick one. But then, why would I be here? Perhaps they just think I have some disease.

Doña María says good afternoon and they stand waiting, shifting their weight from one foot to another, sighing here and there.

A door opens abruptly.

"Next!" calls the doctor, whose head is half bald. He says goodbye to two women. A man in a shiny suit gets up and follows behind him, and the young Indian girl approaches Doña María with a card in her hand.

As her mother digs in her coin purse, Nefer feels the fear reawaken inside her, growing, and her stomach tightens.

The ray of sunlight that shone onto the ceiling has crept down the wall by the time the doctor opens the door and says:

"Ma'am."

Nefer thinks the world is ending and maybe her legs won't respond, but her body propels her to follow her mother, who greets the doctor, nodding her head several times. He shows them into the office and closes the door.

"Sit down. You came for . . ."

Doña María points without looking:

"For her."

"Mm-hmm . . ."

The doctor looks at Nefer:

"What is it that you have . . . ?"

"Doctor, she claims . . ." Doña María's voice breaks into a wail and she starts to cry as her fingers search her pockets for a handkerchief. The doctor puts a hand on her shoulder:

"Calm down, ma'am," and turning back to Nefer: "what seems to be the problem?"

Nefer looks at the cuffs of his pants grazing against his polished shoes and she clears her throat:

"I'm pregnant."

"Nefer!" her mother protests, sobbing into her handkerchief. "That's what she says. Is it true? . . . And she's been throwing up, but I just don't believe it . . . Although she's so troublesome . . . so troublesome . . ."

"Let's see, please get undressed," the doctor says.

The room blurs for Nefer and the details swell: the edge of her dress, a leg and a shoe, another leg and its shoe, her hair in her face, the cold, dry hand palpating her belly.

The doctor breathes deeply and straightens up, he walks over to an autoclave sterilizer and takes out a rubber glove which he starts to put on.

Time has stopped in this room where the women's eyes avoid each other and a faucet drips ceaselessly.

Nefer sees that the doctor is rubbing Vaseline on the index finger of the glove, and her terrified soul retreats into other worlds: she finds herself remembering the pattern of a dress from her childhood, the little white flowers with red in the center. The doctor approaches and says something to her, she obeys but thinks of her horse – Doña María is watching – her dapple horse that Doña María watches, and the doctor here smelling of cologne, her horse of green grass, her horse eating the grass, the green grass, so glad her horse is resting, not like Nefer. Oh, this doctor, this doctor, how she hates him and her mother and the stupid canary outside cheeping and hopping about as if everything were right with the world.

"Mm-hmm . . ." says the man and he stands up. "Get dressed and go wait outside for a moment, all right?"

Nefer puts on her clothes with clumsy movements and feels as if her eyes will never again be able to look up. Once more she feels listless, her blood thick as mud, and when the doctor opens the door she walks out into the front room where an old man is waiting.

Perhaps the doctor will say they're wrong and that Nefer has nothing more than fatigue and sadness. Her eyes clear up at the thought.

"You can come back in."

She sees her mother holding the handkerchief to her nose, aware that under that mask of sorrow her eyes are livid.

"As I was saying to your mother . . ." starts the doctor.

Nefer is not interested because she can't understand his words, and lowering her head she stares down at Doña María's shabby shoes.

The blinds have been lowered, darkening the inside of the café. They sip their sodas without speaking to one another. Nefer takes a sip and her eyes fall on her mother's hand resting next to the glass, and the mere sight of this composure fills her with silent desperation.

Behind the counter a man arranges some glasses.

"Tomorrow it'll all be over," says Doña María.

"What . . . ?"

"Tomorrow we'll be done with all this. You'll see."

A new fear takes hold of Nefer and suddenly she feels as if the enemy shadowing her night and day has become a secret ally. She crosses her arms sullenly.

"Nobody's going to lay a finger on me . . ." she says.

Doña María looks at her:

"Ah, no?"

"No."

She knows that her mother is bursting with rage and that the barman's presence is the only thing saving her.

"You're so stupid . . ."

Without responding, she takes another sip.

Her former tormenter has become her friend, her companion in a private world, which, until only a few days ago, was untainted by outside words and prying eyes. Her blood thins and begins to flow freely through her body, her mouth softens. She's no longer alone.

She finds Doña María intolerable and gets up:

"I'm going to the bathroom."

In the tiny room she's surprised by her own dull gaze looking back at her from the mirror. She smooths down her mousy hair, pinches her cheeks, and smiles.

The sound of a car stopping outside and two doors slamming shut.

Nefer looks at her thin arms, her neck dark and frail, and tries, on her tiptoes, to see the reflection of her whole figure, but the mirror is small and hung high. So she traces her hands down her sides and sighs.

The memory of the doctor returns and her face burns with shame. She hates him, how she hates him – and her mother, who witnessed her humiliation with eyes of stone. She would prefer to stay in this fetid and sweltering bathroom rather than go out and face her mother, the bus that will be waiting outside the hotel in two hours, and everything else.

But she's tired of standing so she leaves. At the table, her mother is talking with Doña Mercedes and, beyond them, Luisa has chosen a table. Doña María has her handkerchief at her eyes, she shakes her head, cries, and keeps talking. Fat Doña Mercedes is also shaking her head, leaning in, and saying something.

Nefer takes a step back, keeping her eyes on them: her mother shakes her head a few more times and dabs at her eyes while the patrona rests a hand on her shoulder and speaks emphatically. Then Doña Mercedes kisses her mother on the cheek and walks away.

Nefer approaches, and although she knows her godmother and Luisa are watching, she pretends not to notice so she doesn't have to say hello.

10

Her heart is heavy as she navigates the puddles, and, espadrilles in hand, she arrives at the base of the wind pump.

All day the land has burned beneath the sun, and now the evening wanes into a burgundy haze. The tracks of the automobile that brought them back from the city are still visible on the path. A fine mist from the water tank cools Nefer as she works the pump until a fresh sparkling stream gushes out onto her arms and face and neck.

The water revives her.

Another day she would have felt joy. Not today. By now the discovery of her silent friend has lost its novelty. On the trip back she carried it with her like a secret, and when she entered her room and sat down on the bed she still felt it there.

But as Alcira was buttoning up a luminous new blouse and admiring herself in the mirror, Nefer furtively observed her sister's gestures as she let her hair loose, the wry smile as she did up the buttons, her pale arms raised.

What does it mean to carry around a secret friend? The other girls go to parties wearing luminous blouses, and they admire themselves smugly in the mirror, and when they get married they go live on their own with their husbands, far away from their parents. How could she have felt pleased with herself in that dirty bathroom at the bar? There are no secret friends here. A sad seed that grows and grows mercilessly, that's what she's carrying around – not a secret friend.

And to think her mother had offered to . . .

She places one foot on the first rung of the wind pump; her hands and feet alternate as she climbs and when she gets to the top she steps over the railing and sits down. She sees the sheep tramping home one after another among the thistles, and a flock of birds sails through the sky like a silent arrow into the reddish clouds.

To think that Doña María had suggested . . .

Carefully she begins her descent. Then she walks toward the house where the radio chatters and Alcira is preparing dinner because their mother has laid down to rest her feet.

Nefer peeks into the bedroom.

"Mamá . . ."

"What!"

"Were you sleeping?"

"No. What is it?"

"You . . ."

Her mother sighs irritably; she sits up and lights a candle. Then she turns, feigning excessive patience.

"What do you want? Well, don't just stand there! If you have something to say then say it, otherwise . . ."

"Mamá, you said today that . . . that tomorrow you were going to take me to . . . to get rid of everything . . ."

"Me . . . ? I said that because I was angry, but it can't actually be done. The police would take you away."

"The police? What about Doña Lola? Why didn't they take her? And Paula . . . ?"

"Anyway. It's not allowed. Go on, get out."

"But you said . . ."

"'You said, you said' – and what about *you*? What did *you* say? . . . Do you remember what you said? Do you? *Nobody's going to lay a finger on me*, that's what you said. Remember now? So, you're going to have to live with it. She who goes out looking for a good time has to pay the price . . ."

"No. No. I'm not just going to live with it. I'll go to Old Lady Borges's house if you won't help me. I'll go to Paula's, otherwise I'll kill myself, that'll make you happy. You want me dead, don't you? That's it. I'll kill myself, and then they'll send you to jail anyway! Just you wait and see . . . Just you wait and see . . ."

"Don't be stupid! Just shut up, will you? Or do you think we're idiots? Everything will get worked out, you'll see . . . But shut up! Don't yell! Get out of here and don't let me see your face again!"

Nefer slams the door and runs off.

From Juan's room comes a reddish glow shining across the floor. Nefer stops to watch him hunched over at work on something, his guitar beside him.

He looks up.

"Hello . . ."

Nefer's face is like clay.

"What are you doing?" she asks.

Juan holds up a small silver medallion:

"Your father gave me this."

"As a gift?"

"Uh-huh."

"Are you putting it on your belt?"

"Yep."

She watches him attach the medallion to the belt using thin strips of rawhide.

"Do you have a lot of them?"

Juan holds up the belt.

"Just five for now, but I'm going to keep adding more."

"Why don't you use ten-cent coins and then swap them out one by one?"

"Not my style."

There's a silence and he says:

"You went into town . . ."

"Yes . . ."

"You got a ride back in a motorcar, huh?"

"Yes."

"Are you all right?"

"Not so great."

"Oh . . ."

Nefer drags her foot back and forth along the floor:

"Juan . . ."

"Yeah?"

"Remember yesterday when you asked if I needed help?"

"Yeah."

"No one can help me."

"Your mother told Don Pedro that everything was already taken care of."

They both blush. It's the first time the subject has come up and Nefer isn't sure how much Juan knows.

"What did she say?" she asks.

"I was in the barn and I heard your mother telling Don Pedro that the patrona was going to take care of your problem. That's all she said."

"The patrona?"

"Yep."

"But. How?"

"I don't know, I don't . . ."

Nefer remembers her mother speaking with Doña Mercedes at the table in the bar.

"But, what's the patrona going to do?"

"Um . . . what do I know?"

"And Mamá just went ahead and blurted it out for anyone to hear . . ."

Juan nods timidly. Nefer looks down at the floor.

"Okay . . . See you . . ." she murmurs.

"See you."

As Nefer walks across the patio with a basket of clean clothes hitched against the side of her hip she sees Don Pedro trimming down a horse's tattered mane. She stops and sets her load on the ground.

She watches the gentle struggle of the ears that twitch in an attempt to escape the shears, and how Don Pedro spits into his palms once he's finished with the mane and then kneels down to trim the hooves with quick clips. Over and over the blade splits off slivers that lie still in the dust. These sounds, these steady movements, soothe Nefer. The sun gently warms her shoulders.

Don Pedro glides to the other side of the horse and carefully tries to repeat the operation, but the horse won't let him get near, kicking restlessly.

Nefer watches the scene with reverence. Her father talks to the horse and nuzzles him until he's calmed down. Then he says in a low voice:

"Someone who doesn't know any better would say he's skittish . . . But it's not right to speak of something you're ignorant about . . ."

Nefer nods in silence; they both know the animal was spooked once when he got caught in some barbed wire.

"And so it goes . . ." says Don Pedro. "It's not right to go around talking just for the sake of having something to say . . . Lots of times it's just a question of bad luck . . ."

Nefer feels her heart skip a beat and tears well up in her eyes, blinding her. She forces them open, fighting back the tears, and only then does she notice that Don Pedro hasn't even looked up from his task.

"Isn't that the case?" he murmurs.

"Mm-hmm . . ."

"That's why, when things have gone sour, there's no sense in making 'em worse . . . Better to keep moving forward . . . just keep moving."

Nefer looks at her father bent down under the shadow of his hat. There's a moment of silence and she falters. Then she whispers:

"But when things happen . . ."

"Huh?"

"When something happens . . . something that's gonna come . . ."

"Nothing's so bad . . . Things come and then they're here."

His sweet words melt her anguish for a moment. Life is easy when you look at it this way. Almost easy.

Doña María peers from the doorway and calls out.

"You still haven't hung the laundry . . ."

"No."

"I don't want you going out this afternoon. We've got visitors coming. Put on some decent clothes after siesta."

"But I've got to . . ."

"Juan'll do it. Now hang out those clothes."

"Who's coming?"

But her mother has gone back inside. Don Pedro leads the horse away slowly, tying her under the shade of a tree.

Even though she was defiant. Even though she refused to take a nap or to put on "some decent clothes." Even though after lunch she went out walking in the brush in a stupor, and she got stuck with a thorn, and she stopped to look at a spider web. Despite all this, siesta still hadn't ended by the time she got back, and she was exhausted. She slept for ten minutes and changed into a nice dress. Alcira is in a foul mood, and Nefer doesn't dare ask her about the visitors.

She walks outside, and, sitting on a bench, she blankly watches some ants devouring a geranium.

These visitors will no doubt be the patrona with a doctor or a nurse, a mammoth nurse with a stiff hairnet and soft shoes like she saw years ago in the hospital.

The idea of being freed makes her sad again. These people, with their meddling ways, barging in to manhandle the silent friend who fills her days – this doesn't cheer her up.

But it's silly to think of it as a friend. What's gotten into her head? It's not a friend, it's a burden. A burden, she knows it's a burden, but why should she depend on others? Others who come in to settle everything with their solemn, knowing faces.

It doesn't matter what happens: to be free again, free from all this.

How? Didn't Doña María say the police would take her away? Secret problems can't be solved by patrones because they don't understand. Patrones and police think in the same way.

No. She was wrong. Why didn't she remember this earlier? Her godmother told her that having an abortion – that's the word – is worse than a crime, because it's killing someone who can't defend themself. Time has passed since her godmother spoke those words, but she can hear them again clearly now: "You think that just because we haven't seen its face, there's no harm in killing it?"

So the patrona would never bring a doctor.

Now Nefer feels hollowed out by this great deception.

She had resolved to defend herself against them. But evidently she had also hoped to become free. All right. The patrona will fix the problem. But, if she's not bringing a doctor, what's there to fix?

Suddenly she knows. She presses her lips together. She knows, but it won't work; she won't say anything. They'll bring the priest. Their visit will be futile. They'll bring him to make Nefer confess. Yes, but they're mistaken. Doña Mercedes and the priest, and Nefer greeting them, and Doña Mercedes leaving her alone with the priest so Nefer will confess. That's it! But she won't . . . Or . . . Maybe she will confess. She will. Yes, and the sin will leave her.

But, what about the other thing? It — she — is not going to disappear with a simple confession.

That's what her godmother means by "taking care of the problem."

The ants have stripped the geranium leaf bare. Beyond the gate comes the sound of an automobile, and before she can think Nefer stands and runs out into the brush. She sees car doors and wheels flash between the trees. They pass by and disappear and then she hears sounds coming from the kitchen.

She turns to hear better and can picture her mother: fat, her face covered in powder, grimacing to greet the priest. Oh, if only she had a horse and could escape forever.

She presses her cheek against a tree and waits.

But Don Pedro must be there, sitting politely and waiting for Nefer to appear. She stares at the branches to let some more time pass before she has to act. She'll go back, for her father's sake.

Her palms turn clammy as she approaches. She wants to listen without being seen, the sharp gushing voice of her godmother, the saccharine tone of her mother, the priest's voice booming above all the others — the same one that echoed against the walls of the chapel during his sermon.

But there is no priest's voice and the kitchen is quiet. The patrona says abruptly:

"How about this weather! Do you think it will rain?"

Someone says something in response. Another moment of silence and Doña Mercedes speaks again:

"What a lovely calendar! The last one had that horrendous picture of a cyclist. I like this one much better."

"Oh, yes," says Nefer's mother; "it comes along free with the seed catalog, they give 'em out."

"Oh . . . And tell me, Doña María, this kitchen stove of yours, does it work alright?"

"Um . . . yes ma'am . . . it's good. It's . . . what I mean is . . . well, this one suits me just fine."

A new voice, thick with tobacco, says:

"These chimneys are the best. They've got a flue . . . If it's all right with you I'll just take a look . . ."

She doesn't recognize that voice. Could it be the doctor? It's not the priest. She's scared; perhaps they've come to take her away to a hospital with bars and gray walls.

From behind her the same voice says:

"Hello there . . ."

As she turns around her eyes trip over a chest and move up to a face dominated by a mustache. It takes her a moment to place him.

Nicolás, the one who worked on the railway, holds out a clumsy hand:

"How've you been . . ."

"Alright . . ."

There's a silence and he points to the roof:

"I came out to look at the chimney . . ."

He stands there, his hand still pointing. Then he says:

"What a miracle, don't you think? Funny thing about life . . ."

"What's that?"

"Um . . . that we should find ourselves here today, after so long . . ."

Nefer looks up at him and notices his eyes on her belly. In a jolt, that night, the scent of wine, the gasps, they all come back to her. What fills her is more than memory; she is reliving it once again.

He says quickly in a thick voice:

"Listen . . ."

"What."

"You're sure it's mine, right? Because if you're not . . . Are you sure?"

Nefer shrugs. For an instant she's tempted to pretend she doesn't know what he's talking about. How does he know? But she answers without looking at him:

"Who else's would it be?"

After a silence the man laughs:

"Funny thing about life . . . full of surprises." And he spits.

Nefer feels the heat of the sun coming off the thatched roof. She murmurs:

"Why?"

"What do you mean, why? Who would have thought that we . . . that so soon . . . so soon, no? That we'll be married . . . Who would have thought?"

Nefer raises her eyes and scans his rosy cheeks, his forehead, his droopy whiskers. He leans one hand on the wall.

"If you're good and hardworking, I don't mind. I'm a good guy, too. Sometimes I lose my temper, but I get over it soon enough . . . You know what I mean, right? I'm working at the butcher shop now, lots of knives, lots of sawing. You can't be squeamish 'cause sometimes I come home with my arms stained up to here . . . But we'll be in town, and really you'll be better off than you are here . . . Why, you're a young one, aren't you? Who would have thought . . . Ain't that something, I apologize, but wine will do that . . . And in the end, in the end, you didn't have such a bad time either, did you now? I mean . . ."

He winks, laughing, and scratches the back of his neck.

"But . . . who would have thought? My whole life I've been crazy about big blonde girls, and now this. Whattaya know . . . I'm gettin' married to a little dark-haired girl of a thing. Life's a mystery . . ."

Her godmother approaches, blinking her eyes in the sun.

"Nefer . . . Oh, what's this? You ran into each other out here? Why don't you come inside? It's so hot out."

Her mother is alone in the kitchen. She pours some mate and holds it out to Nicolás:

"Here you are."

"Excuse me, ma'am, did you add sugar?"

Doña María blushes because her habit of sweetening the yerba has been discovered:

"Yes . . . I did."

"Ah . . . all right then, because I — well, I don't know why, but I drink my mate with sugar. I'm not a true countryman in that way . . ."

He lets out a hearty laugh and slurps noisily.

"Nefer dear," says her godmother, "why don't you go find your father? I'd like to speak with him."

She walks slowly with the dog at her side. She has no voice to call his name and instead looks around.

Don Pedro is cutting strips of leather in the shade of the barn; he holds the rawhide in one hand and slices into it with a knife. The strips curl like little white roots.

"What are you doing?" murmurs Nefer.

"Working, it seems . . ."

"They want to talk to you."

"To me."

"Yes, Doña Mercedes . . ."

"Hmmm."

Don Pedro examines one strip and starts to cut another.

"I'll have to go on in then, won't I . . ."

Nefer asks herself whether he knows. He rolls up the strips and tucks them away, making a gentle gesture of resignation.

"I'll have to go on in, I guess . . ."

11

She stares at the white dress Luisa sent, lifeless on the hanger and worn from use. Then she looks at her mother, who's packing a suitcase with old and new clothes, and at her sister putting on the dazzling blouse.

In the blue air the wind pump turns.

Nefer unfolds a little piece of paper. Her godmother's handwriting is so large that the letters seem to scream at her:

I'll be there. Remember that marriage is a sacrament. If you'd like to confess, the priest is very nice and I've already spoken with him . . .

When she puts on the dress she tries to avoid her reflection in the mirror. Her mother sews a quick stitch and, with a wide ribbon, tries to cinch the dress around Nefer's small frame, but the long skirt tickles her ankles.

"Don't make that face. Don't be silly. Long dresses are in fashion, and it's good quality cloth . . ."

Her bare neck is defenseless and dark.

Afterward, she wanders aimlessly into the sunshine. She looks at the sleepy dapple gray in the corral and the vast trembling grassland filled with the cries of the lapwings. Juan arrives at a trot, and as he greets her he looks away from the dress.

"Here," he says. "I don't have anything else."

It's a silver medallion in the shape of a daisy.

"No," murmurs Nefer. "Keep it. It's from your belt."

"It doesn't look right on my belt. It's a gift, take it."

Nefer looks at the flower shining in her hand.

"It's the only gift I like . . ."

"What else did they give you?"

"This dress and a set of teacups."

"Don't lose it . . . Bye."

He nudges the horse with his heels and is about to set off, but then hesitates and stops.

"Well," he says. "Good luck. Bye, Nefer."

"Bye."

Squeezing the silver flower in her hand, she walks back into the house. Don Pedro, dressed in his Sunday best, is saying:

"If we want to catch the train we'd better leave."

She thinks of how high up the wheels are, of having to climb the steps with these legs saddened by fatigue. Alcira's new blouse gleams in the sunshine.

Riding in a wagon is like skimming over the surface of the earth, viewing the countryside from above while the planks jostle nosily below. Don Pedro holds the reins stiffly in his hands; Nefer sits impassively at his side. Smelling like powder, her mother tucks her legs under her seat and sighs. Behind them, his tongue lolling, panting, Capitán stops now and then to drink from the ditches.

Negro's horse dozes in front of the general store.

Nefer doesn't look. She stares at her hands resting on the white dress clouded with dust.

When the train arrives at the station her mother pushes her up and climbs on behind her, huffing and puffing. From another seat, a man greets Don Pedro and walks over to talk. His voice dissolves into the sound of the train, but Nefer overhears bits of their conversation.

"I figured if I sell I already know I'll end up losing, so I might as well sow my seeds now and after the harvest we'll just have to wait and see . . ."

Nefer glances at the top of her suitcase, at the plains unfolding beyond the dirty window.

"The harvest. From here on out I'll be a married woman when the harvest comes."

Across the aisle, her mother has fallen asleep.